I WAKE UP
SCREAMING

STEVE FISHER

Black Lizard Books

Berkeley • 1988

Steve Fisher was born in 1912, and began his writing career while in the United States Navy from 1928–32. He lived in New York, where he wrote for pulp magazines such as *Pocket Detective, Ellery Queen's Mystery Magazine* and *The Saint,* and published his first crime novels. He later moved to Hollywood where he had a lengthy career as a screen and television writer. Among his screenplays were "Lady in the Lake," "Dead Reckoning," "Tokyo Joe," "I, Mobster" and "Las Vegas Shakedown." His television credits include "Miami Undercover," "McMillan and Wife," "Starsky and Hutch" and "Barnaby Jones." Fisher's most memorable novels are *The Hell-Black Night, Saxon's Ghost* and the famous *I Wake Up Screaming,* which was filmed in 1941, and starred Victor Mature and Betty Grable. Steve Fisher died in 1980.

Copyright © 1960 by Steve Fisher.
I Wake Up Screaming is published by Black Lizard Books, 833 Bancroft Way, Berkeley, CA 94710. Black Lizard Books are distributed by Creative Arts Book Company. For information contact: The Schallert Agency, Inc., 9350 Wilshire Boulevard, Beverly Hills, CA 90212.

Composition by QuadraType, San Francisco.

ISBN 0-88739-085-4
Library of Congress Catalog Card No. 87-71820

Manufactured in the United States of America.

For Mary

Chapter One

It was a hot Saturday night and I had on a Sy Devore suit and a hand-knit tie and sat at the bar in Mike Romanoff's drinking Canadian Club old fashioneds. The bar stools were leather and the wall decorations had that ultra look and Zsa Zsa Gabor was at a closeby table, her head thrown back in laughter, and Gary Cooper and Bing Crosby and Bill Holden were at other tables and a couple of blocks away, on the corner of Wilshire and Beverly Drive, they were having a premiere for the latest Jerry Wald epic: arc lights swinging back and forth, limousines arriving, and cops holding off the crowd. I was at long last in tinsel town and I was excited. At the same time I felt lonely. That sweet, hot loneliness that's like music. I was twenty-seven, had a play on Broadway, and now a studio contract at one of the majors that was still making big wide screen pictures. Hell, I even had my Writer's Guild of America card! I thought about things. Those first hard years were over. This was it, I thought. *This is the works!*

On Monday morning I reported to the studio for work. The story editor was a nice guy. He wore glasses, was very casual, called me by my first name, said not to worry much about learning the screen play form, and to beware of local scenarists, because most Hollywood writers hated the very guts of a New York importation. After that he said I should stand by for an assignment, and gave me a load of shooting scripts to read to while away the time. He conducted me to a nice big office with a couch and brown Venetian blinds. From there on I was on my own.

For days I was afraid to leave the office because the thought haunted me that while I was out a producer might ring. I read all of the scripts. One written by Ben Hecht was a honey. I ate big lunches and took naps on the couch. I

1

became so bored that I began to practice pitching pennies against the wall. I developed a twist of the wrist technique and became quite excellent at it. Later, I used to prop my door open—so I could hear the phone if it rang—and wander forlornly up and down the hall.

It was in the hall that I first saw Vicky Lynn.

I stopped cold in my tracks. My first thought was that she was some star who, by mistake, had gotten lost up here in the Writers' Jungle. But she was a secretary. Her hair was golden blond like the Marchand ad and came to her shoulders. She was wearing a soft, pleated blue skirt, and her hips had a nice, exquisite swing. Her breasts were nippled sharply against a white middy blouse. But all the same she was like A Creature—a lovely baby. I heard her laugh that day, warm, rich laughter, and I shivered.

The second time I saw her she was in the switchboard reception room on the writers' floor. Secretaries often go in there with marked up shorthand books and worn down pencils and flop limply into the nearest chair. Writers go in to read the switchboard girl's afternoon paper. I went in and sat down. Vicky was so near I could have touched her, but I didn't know what to say, how to start a conversation. I didn't want to louse things up. She was talking to someone else and she glanced at me only once. After a while she left.

My spirit got up and went with her. What was left of me sat there in the chair in a sweet daze.

I rode down in the elevator that night with Lanny Craig. He was a big guy with thick eyebrows, graying hair and a limp; but he imagined himself still a boy. In between picture assignments he wrote English mysteries which were second rate imitations of Agatha Christie. He had started out in Greenwich Village, but he was not what even *he* would call a success. Here at the studio he was in the B Unit of a notorious exploitation-type executive who ground out films on a hundred-thousand dollar budget aimed at drive-in theaters and teen-age audiences—horror, sex and outer space. He said pictures used to be bad in the old days, but they were great compared to what he was now writing. He told me there was no middle area in picture making any more. They either made *Suddenly Last Summer* or *Beatnik in a*

Hot Rod. He was wearing slacks, an open shirt and a sports coat.

"I'm having some people over Sunday—want to make it?"

"I'll try," I said. "Listen, that's really a babe upstairs, isn't it?"

"Who—Vicky Lynn?"

"Is that her name?"

"Yeah, Vicky Lynn." He laughed. "A cat can look at heaven, of course—but if you've an idea you can make Vicky it's a very sad thing indeed." The elevator door clanged open. "We've all tried, kid."

"What's the matter—has she got a guy?"

"The girls say no. It's just no dice."

On Friday I talked to Vicky for the first time. We were in the switchboard room, and I said something about the weather, and then I asked her if she had ever thought of writing a story. It was the old line. She said she'd written a story, or was writing one. I was too excited to get it straight. I remember she promised she would let me see what it was she had written.

For three days nothing happened. Then she came in, shyly, a four-page thing in her hand. She put it on my desk and mumbled something about it being awfully kind of me to want to read it. Our eyes met only once, and she flushed, embarrassed, and I thought: She knows, and I know, that this is a game, and in the end it will mean a date. When she had been gone only an hour I telephoned her and said that I wanted to discuss the story. I said it would be better if we talked outside of the studio. She hesitated, and I pretended it made no difference to me. "All right, then," I said, "never mind." That was when she agreed to meet me.

I picked her up on a street corner and we went to the Beachcomber. We had a side table and the lights were soft. Polynesian waiters swished past and there was Island music. It was like something out of James Michener. Vicky sat there shyly, and I was awkward, saying a lot of damn fool things that echoed back in my ears, whispering revision, papa, these things you say may be true but they have a

3

phony ring. You know how it is sometimes with a girl that's really terrific. I couldn't get started. My fingers walked back and forth on the tablecloth. The waiter came and I ordered Zombies. There's nothing like a nice warm jag to break the ice.

It worked! About halfway through the first Zombies we were doing swell. Vicky laughed in sheer relief, and now she was gorgeous. Candlelight flickered on the table, and very softly and eloquently she began to recite little snatches of poetry. Wistful little verses. She was just a kid. I was charmed. I began to talk like a love scene.

"Gosh, you're swell! Where've you been?"

Two More Zombies!

"You're beautiful, Vicky! You're ineffable!"

"I'm what?"

"You're tops, honey. You're silk stockings from Paris; you're Shelley on a moonlit night."

"You aren't exactly fat and bald yourself," she said.

"Sure I am; it's just the cut of my clothes that deceives you."

"You're the youngest writer in the studio—except for the fifty dollar a week junior writers. Did you know I noticed you that first day in the switchboard room?"

"You only think that was the first day," I said. "I've been following you around, up and down halls, across the lot, like—"

"I'd—rather you didn't say like what."

I laughed.

"I want you to know," she said, "that from the first time our eyes met—I thought you were swell!" She put down her drink. "Oh, but we're starting the wrong way! A girl doesn't tell a man what she thinks—and she—she doesn't get drunk before dinner. Even in Hollywood! We're going to spoil everything, aren't we?"

"Of course not!"

"But we will! People always tell polite lies to each other at first—and we've been so frank, it's—embarrassing. You'll hate me!"

"Sure," I said, "I'll hate you in heaven!"

"I'm just a silly, romantic fool," she said. "But it never

4

happened this way before, and—oh, that sounds so old, doesn't it?"

"That's the trouble with love," I said, "—it's old." We were merrier than Disney's mice by now. "Look, shall we have dinner?"

"All right."

"Here—or elsewhere? Name your favorite hash house, Vicky."

"It doesn't matter," she said. Then: "Would you like me to cook? We might disgrace a restaurant by tripping over a table or something. I'll cook for you if you want."

"Ah—a girl scout!"

But it was a lovely idea. We left the Beachcomber and I somehow navigated my car to her apartment. It was a place on Franklin—you know, the stone statue on the lawn spurting water into a goldfish pond—and she shared two rooms on the fourth floor with her sister. It was average. About $80 a month. There were knickknacks around, a portable radio, and a pretty, gaudy rag doll that sat on the floor, its head askew. Vicky went in ahead of me and I helped her with her coat.

She went into the bedroom then. After a while I followed her. She was standing in front of the mirror putting on lipstick with her little finger. She turned around, and all at once I was kissing her. I don't know how long we stood there kissing. But she wasn't just any girl. I knew that she was the one I'd been dreaming about.

We were very tight. She wore a soft gray dress, I remember that; and my hand started roving. It wasn't right. I didn't want her to think I was a cheap heel—that this was everything. She began to cry, and was sort of fighting, and crying.

Then it was all right.

Afterward, I stood at the window. The room was dark and you could see the street below. I heard Vicky crying, softly—broken-hearted. I called myself a louse, the way you do. I had a hell of a headache.

I went out through the living room and into the kitchenette. I turned on the faucet and ducked my head under it, then wiped my face with a dirty dish towel. There was a pot

5

with a little stale coffee in it and I lit the fire under it. When it was hot I drank it black, and shook my head. There was no sound from the other room. I lit a cigarette and stood there, trembling.

I looked around the kitchen, opening cupboards. I found some chops, and began making dinner. I had never cooked dinner in my life. I put on an apron. Once I went in to see about Vicky. She'd imagined I'd left. She was sobbing. I crept back into the kitchen and finished the dinner—cutting my finger on a tin can and scorching the potatoes. But when the food was all on the table it looked fine.

I got a damp cloth from the bathroom and went into the bedroom and applied it to Vicky's forehead, and wiped away all the tears. She was staring up at me, through the dark. I got her to stand up, and she came out to the kitchen in her stockings. She stared at the dinner that was cooling, and then she looked at me. She couldn't quite believe it. I pulled back a chair.

"Voulez-vous?"

She sat down and I scrambled into the built-in seat opposite her. She had sobered considerably, and she was cute. We had a post-mortem, of course. "You must think I'm awful!" It wasn't time to be flip or I would have said, no, she was lovely. It turned out that she had once been engaged. It was all over now, but the affair had lasted a long time, and she'd been really in love. "And there was no one else—ever!" She told it straight, and I knew, in some way, that it was the God's truth. She was intensely sincere. I got away from the subject. I made some pointless sally or other, and she laughed.

"You're such an elegant guy!" she said.

"And you're such a pretty baby, gee—"

"No." She shook her head. "It's my sister that's pretty. She sings with a band. You'll have to meet her."

"I certainly will."

"She's three years older than I am—I'm twenty-two—and not engaged or anything." She paused, engrossed. "Of course—she's chased by Paul. Quite terrifically. He's our community millionaire. Every blonde knows one. He bores Jill. But what can you do? One Sunday when she wouldn't see him he sent over roast pheasant and champagne—

6

imagine Jill and I sitting here alone, eating a dinner like that!" She looked up. "And he's an awful cheat. Once we hung a dress on a mop just to see if it was true he'd go for anything in skirts."

"Was he insulted?"

"So much that the next day he sent Jill a mink coat—she returned it, of course. She's like that. She wouldn't have Paul on toast!"

"Would you have returned the coat?"

Vicky laughed. "I don't know!" She went on: "I don't think Jill's ever been really in love. Yet—she *is* emotional. I suppose one day she'll fall in love so hard she'll never get over it. Am I boring you?"

"In an enchanting sort of way."

"What a silly person I am! I'll drive you from the place screaming!"

We finished the coffee and went into the other room. I sat with the long-legged rag doll on my lap, the radio playing low, and asked all about her. She had been raised in Los Angeles and was a graduate of Hollywood High School. She showed me her class ring and I swiped it and put it on my little finger.

"Token," she said.

She was radiantly beautiful.

"How come you took a studio job?"

"I always wanted to get in the movies. I thought that might be a way."

"Is it?"

"Apparently not. But a director took me to dinner once."

"Who?"

"His name is Hurd Evans."

"What was wrong?"

"He—well, you know how it is. And I—I just couldn't stand him."

"The heel." I looked up at her. "Listen—you're marvelous, see? You'll get in pictures and it won't have to be through the back door."

I was just talking. But it suddenly occurred to me that I had struck upon something. I felt a quick surge of excitement. Here was Vicky who had everything: beauty and personality and music in her voice. She said she'd been in a few amateur plays and had done all right. It was possible that there were strings I could pull in the studio. Certainly I could afford to back her with a little money!

"I'm going to see about it," I said.

She frowned. "Look, baby, you're so sweet—*you* don't have to say that. Everybody out here makes promises. Just be you, that's all."

"Yes—sure, but—you've got the groceries, Vicky! With a little grooming—it's personalities they want and—you know, I really think—"

I ran away with myself. We began talking about it. I told her I was going to do everything I could. I'd hire a press agent. I'd send her to dramatic school. We'd get her in the Community Playhouse. We'd have dozens of photographs made. I'd get an agent to take her around to the studios. I knew an artist who'd paint her for a magazine cover. Then I thought of the idea of getting a couple of guys to go in with me as her sponsors. That would be the ticket!

She was a star when I finished talking. We were shouting promotion ideas back and forth. We acted out bits of scenes we remembered from pictures. We walked up and down the room reading Shakespeare.

"How'm I doing, baby?"

"Fine, Juliet. You're simply swell. Aren't you swell, though?"

Suddenly we had stopped the rehearsal and I was holding her in my arms. It was two in the morning. She clung to me and whispered she loved me, and she was crying. I laughed because I was happy. I kissed her warm lips. I told her she was Cinderella.

Chapter Two

I met her sister the next day. It was Saturday and I came up at noon. Jill was there. She wore a blue lounging robe and there wasn't any make-up on her face, but she was pretty. Her hair was yellow and came short of her shoulders. She was slender, taller than Vicky. I had a little florist's box in my hand but I stopped in the middle of the room and stared at her. She looked at me the same way. For a moment I felt a chill. She looked *very* familiar. It was as though I should kiss her and say, *Darling, I've been a long time away. How are you?* But then it passed. I imagine it'd just been that she resembled Vicky. When she spoke her voice was pleasant. It was a low, very soft voice.

"Hello. Vicky's talked about you all night and half the morning. How are you?"

"Fine," I said. "I'm glad to know you, Jill."

Vicky came in then, wearing white silk slacks, and I gave her the florist's box. She opened it, very carefully, and then she took out the flower. It was a white orchid with a deep scarlet center. Vicky gazed at it tenderly. She looked at me, and then she looked over at Jill.

"That's funny," she said. "Nobody *ever* bought me a *white* orchid!"

"What's it for?" said Jill. "You two going out?"

"I don't know." My cheeks were hot. "I was just walking along and saw a shop and went in and bought it. I don't know what it's for."

Jill sat down. She had the morning paper. I looked at her.

"I understand you sing?"

"A little."

"I always wanted to meet a torch singer."

"That isn't what you call it," Jill said. "That's old." She seemed nervous. She kept watching me. It was the damnedest thing I've ever experienced. Vicky went into the kitchen to get a vase for the flower. Jill rumpled the paper.

"You two go ahead. Don't mind me. I've got to pick a horse. I always bet on Saturdays. Do you know a horse?"

"I'm sorry," I said. "I don't."

I followed Vicky into the kitchen. She had placed the orchid in a little glass vase and was still admiring it.

"Hello, starlet," I said.

"We went crazy last night, didn't we?"

"No. I meant it."

She shook her head. "I slept on it. It *couldn't* come true! It's too nice!"

9

I grinned. "You wait, Vicky!"

The three of us went to lunch.

"Paul wanted me to go to the races," Jill said, "but—to be candid—he leaves me cold." She smiled. "Vicky's afraid I'll never fall in love!"

We had gone to the Bali, which was cool and intimate, and empty at this hour. The bartender was polishing glasses, and after a long time a handsome young Polynesian waiter came to our table and smiled, and fixed his pencil, waiting for our order.

We drank cocktails and had a fine lunch. Vicky was perfectly swell. She seemed kind of proud of me. But—I don't know why—I felt strange with Jill there. She was quiet and reserved. The things she said were pleasant and her mood was gay. Yet there was something about her that haunted my imagination. Like a pretty song—she disturbed my emotions. She left early.

"I really must run," she said. "The band rehearses at three. It's been very nice meeting you."

"I didn't know there was a rehearsal this afternoon," Vicky said naïvely.

"But there is, darling. Didn't I tell you?"

Then she was gone.

I was with Vicky all weekend and when I arrived at the studio at ten o'clock on Monday I felt fine. The story editor called me in and said the screen play they'd sent for me to polish had been temporarily shelved and he had a much better job. They had just bought a story. It was about winter in Paris. An American boy and a French girl are trapped in the city when the Nazis marched in. They were hungry, they were haunted; the nights were cold and bitter. It was poignant and beautiful. In the end the girl died. It was magnificent! I was to do the shooting script.

The story editor blew his nose. He had reached the zenith of his emotions.

"I won't see you any more," he said. "From now on you'll work directly with your producer. But I'll always know what you're doing. By option time," he went on ominously, "there'll be a dozen reports about you on my desk.

One thing more. Always remember that your conduct is unimportant. Nobody's got a stop watch on you. You can play craps or go to the races or spend your time in Malibu. Writers in Hollywood work on the merit system. They know if their script is lousy that'll be the end. Nothing counts except your dialogue, continuity and timing. Everything you write will be made up in carbons and read by a dozen people—and we can smell a phony or forced script a mile away. Out here we pay for and get the best writing talent in the world. But a lot of the boys think they don't have to produce—they're wrong!"

As I followed him into the hall, and up the stairs to the producer's office, I felt all noble and full of stirring resolutions. The producer was in his shirt sleeves. He was short, with dark curly hair, and fairly young. Until three months ago he had been a writer. I had heard rumor that now, as a producer, he was the Front Office pet. The story editor went through very solemn formalities and the producer stood twirling a pencil in his hand and looking me over.

When the story editor was gone the producer lay down on his couch and crossed his legs and looked at the ceiling.

"It's hot as hell, ain't it?"

"Yeah," I said, "it's a scorcher."

"This is a conference," said the producer. "Did Al tell you about the story?"

"A little."

The producer turned over on his stomach and began picking threads out of a cushion. "It's a helluva sweet story. If we work it right I think we can get the best stuff out of *A Summer Place* and *Farewell to Arms* and work it all right in. I'll get prints of these films and in a couple of days we'll go to the projection room and look them over. They both grossed like hell, you know."

"They had fine reviews."

"Reviews and grosses ain't always the same thing. You've got to pull in the sticks to make money. New York and all the rest of the big cities put together'd never make up production costs for you. We're going to spend three million on this picture, and do it in Technicolor. We're going to try and borrow Audrey Hepburn from Paramount and Marlon Brando, if he can get any free time, for the lead rôles—but we probably won't get them. My first idea was Debbie Reynolds. But I just talked to her on the phone and she said no soap. Maybe we'll get Gina Lollabrigida for the part. It's a sweet story."

"It certainly is."

He sat up and ran his hands through his curly hair and yawned.

"Well, you take the script and break it down and do me a forty-page treatment," he said. "After that we'll do a sixty-page treatment—and then a first rough draft of the screen play. Most screen plays are exactly a hundred and twenty pages. We'll run ours to a hundred and fifty so the front office can cut it down without killing it."

"All right," I said, "I'll do the treatment."

"How soon'll you have it done—about six weeks?"

"In about ten days," I said.

"You're nuts to write that fast, but it's okay by me."

I went to the commissary for lunch. I had the original story with me, and I wasn't in the commissary at all. I was in a sidewalk café on the Boul' Mich. I was in an attic overlooking the Seine and I held Vicky up to the window because Vicky was sick, and I told her it was our Paris out there and if she listened she could still hear the chimes in Notre Dame Cathedral. I glanced up then and Vicky was really there. She was sitting at a table with two secretaries. I went back to my office and wrote at white hot speed on a typewriter until it got dark outside and the studio cop came around locking doors, and the switchboard girl asked me if I wanted a night trunk line.

I called Vicky and told her I was going to be busy. But I didn't do any more work after all. I was restless and excited and I drove down to Los Angeles and walked the streets, thinking about the story. I was on Main Street and I stood in front of a burlesque show for a while, debating whether I could think better inside; but then I moved on and pretty soon I was looking into a hock shop window. I saw a pair of ancient brass knucks. They might have had value, or a history of which the pawnshop keeper was unaware, and remembering a friend in New York who collected items like this it occurred to me that these would make a good Christmas present. So I went in and bought them and put them in my pocket. I got back into my new Lincoln and drove to Vicky's apartment on Franklin Avenue.

There was a kid at the switchboard half asleep. He was big, and he had a face like cold cream. He wore heavy, thick-lens glasses, and his eyes were monstrous—or so it seemed—behind them. They were round, yellow eyes, and he turned and stared at me blankly. I looked over my shoulder to see whether it was me he was looking at or an escaped gorilla. It was me.

"Well?" he said. His hands were huge and hairy.

"I'd like to see Vicky Lynn."

His face worked. "At this hour?"

I said: "What do I need—your permission?"

He plugged in angrily. But when Vicky came on his voice was honey. I whispered my name just in time. "Shall I throw him out?" he asked.

"Try it, you son of a bitch," I said. But I had my fingers crossed.

He jerked out the plug. "You can go up," he said. The way he looked at me you would have thought I was going upstairs and crawl in bed with his mother.

I found out later that this guy's name was Harry Williams.

"So long, Toots," I said, and I started up the stairs.

Vicky had been preparing for bed and she wore a beautiful black gossamer nightgown and a robe and slim white mules. She said Hey, It's Midnight; then she said But It's All Right, Honey, I'll Keep a Light in the Window and You Just Come Any Hour You Want. So I kissed her. That's a Fine Reward, Baby, she said, I'll Keep Two Lights in the Window, and I kissed her again. I held her very close to me, and kissed her hair, and her neck.

"Oh, baby," she said, "I love you like anything!"

I said: "Some fun, huh, kid?" and she said, "Mmm, boy, I'll say," and I said: "Now to roast some marshmallows."

At one A.M. or a little after we were in the kitchenette sopping up coffee and pushing conversation around. I told her

13

about my run-in downstairs on the switchboard with The Skinny Creep.

"Oh, you mean Harry Williams," she said. "Baby, he isn't quite bright." Then she laughed. "Night before last the manager came home and found him asleep on the board. Poor Harry! You should've heard him crying in his beer. He said he didn't have to work in a joint like this. Let them fire him!"

"Sure. Or let the draft get him."

"No. He said he'd had a card from a distant cousin up in Doris and, by God, he could always get a job up there, by God. A man's job."

"You mean like crocheting sweaters for the Red Cross?"

"Huh-uh. Picking grapes off the vine."

"Oh, Lord!"

Vicky grabbed my hand. "But, listen—this'll kill you dead, baby—Jill thinks Harry has a crush on me!"

"Competition, eh?"

Vicky laughed. We talked a while longer. I was ready to go—had my heart in my hand and everything—when Jill came home. She wore a blue evening gown and she looked terrific in it. Her figure was nice and even. She took my hand.

"Hello, *Pegasus.* How are you, Peg?"

"That's a hell of a name," I said. "I—I was just going, Jill."

"Don't," she said. She talked about the band. "Vicky, the band's going to break up. I don't know how soon." She looked at me. "Don't go yet." But I turned around and kissed Vicky and left. The only hell of it was, it was Jill I was thinking about.

The next morning I looked for Lanny Craig, but his office was empty. The switchboard girl said he was in projection room five and I could either phone him there or go over and see him. He was looking at the old print of a picture called *Hell's Back Door.* I left the building with implicit instructions as to how to get there.

I saw Lanny as soon as I opened the projection room door. There were five rows of seats, all of them empty, and Lanny was sitting in the producer's leather chair in the back of the room. His feet were cocked up, he had a cigar in his mouth, and his hand was operating the control board by which he could signal to have sound volume increased, the picture stopped dead in its frame and re-run, or anything else that struck his notion. At the moment he was experimenting by running the volume up and down just for the hell of it.

He looked over at me just as an old-fashioned gangster scene flashed on. He turned up the sound until it was a roar—on the film it was the shrieking staccato of machine gun bullets. He cut the volume down.

"You're dead," he said. "This morning I am a junior G-man."

I flopped down in a chair beside him.

"I'm doing an epic about gangsters," he said, "or at least with gangsters in it. Stoopenfetchit insisted I sit through this. He said there may be bits we can snip. You know—good old budget. A dime here, a dime there."

"Who's Stoopenfetchit?"

"My producer. You must someday meet the gentleman."

Lanny's face was flabby. He was big, over-grown. He dressed in sloppy clothes, and he wore wrinkled scarfs. But he was a guy I could talk to. He was nuts about women. He could show you addresses and phone numbers. He had each name rated. He was married to an aged, neurotic old woman who had a million dollars and spent half her life in a wheel chair. Lanny said that marriage license was his unemployment insurance policy. The phone from outside rang now and he answered. He placed two bets on the horses and hung up. He had turned the volume on the screen so low that it was like a silent film. The projectionist stuck his head through the square hole behind us.

"Hey—what is this?"

"I'm just looking for long shots we can clip for quick shots in a montage," Lanny replied. "I don't have to listen to that stinking dialogue to do that, do I?"

"I'm looking for a long shot myself," the projectionist said, "—at Santa Anita."

"That's very funny," said Lanny. "You can pull your head back in through that rat hole now if you want."

15

That was another thing about Lanny Craig. He licked the hand of any man he thought made ten dollars a week more than himself, but he was crushing and dirty to inferiors.

"You didn't have to do that," I said. "The guy was just trying to be friendly."

"To hell with him," Lanny said. "Resurrect a Willie Bioff and the projectionists and props men'll be making more than the writers and actors. Comrade, has no one told you of the revolution?"

The film kept flashing grimly from the screen.

"Lanny," I said, "I'm in love."

"Now that Rhonda is single, you mean?"

"It isn't Miss Fleming."

"Poor you!"

I began telling him my idea about sponsoring a girl in pictures. I didn't tell him she was Vicky. But I raved. He puffed on his cigar and kept his eyes on the film. I outlined a few of the plans I had for the campaign and asked him for suggestions.

"What do I get out of it?"

"Nothing, you lecherous bastard. But she *has* got a sister."

"Continue," Lanny said.

I went on and on. We could do this and that. Finally I told him it was Vicky.

"*What?*"

"Yeah. Vicky Lynn. But keep it quiet or she'll get canned."

He didn't believe me. So I showed him the class ring Vicky had given me. He stared. He reached around and patted my back. He asked me how it was. I swore to hell I didn't know and he said I was a liar, but that was all right. "You're a gentleman and a boy scout," he said. And he was interested in the idea. We sat there talking and he got the fever. The picture went off, the screen was blank, the projection room closed up; but we kept talking. We tried to analyze Vicky's defects. We couldn't remember any. She was perfect—merchandise. All we had to do was wrap her in glamour. Lanny picked up the phone and put through an inter-studio call.

"Hurd? Lanny. Meet me in my office, will you, pappy?" He hung up.

"Who's that?"

"Hurd Evans. He directs the pictures I write and he'll go for this idea. He's in a hell of a slump and it'll get him publicity."

"Listen, not him—"

"Why not? He can help us."

"He's a wolf," I said.

"I belong to that club myself," said Lanny.

"Well, he tried to make Vicky."

"And didn't?"

"No. He fell on his face."

"All the better then," Lanny said. "We'll tell him she's your personal property and to lay off. You stick to this virgin story and I'll back you up. It's strictly a business deal. No casting couches. It's damn good business when you can pick up a natural and don't you ever forget old Uncle Lanny told you that."

"How much does Hurd make?"

"Only about two-fifty a week. The guy still carries scissors in his back pocket."

"Scissors?"

"That's right. He was a film cutter last year and he can't break the habit. He knows you were imported from New York and he'll think you're hotter than Tennessee Williams. Tell him you cast your own play on Broadway."

"Okay."

We got up and left the projection room. Lanny spilled cigar ashes on his slacks and stopped to brush them off.

Chapter Three

Hurd Evans wore a three-hundred-dollar gray suit and a white turtle-neck sweater instead of a vest. He was a dandy little guy, with slicked-down brown hair, and an angelic face. I would have said he was about twenty-six. He didn't want it kept a secret that he was a big "Moom

17

Pitcher" director and he dressed to look as Hollywood as possible—but with the select masculinity of a pint-sized Clark Gable. On his wrist he wore a heavy slave bracelet—suggesting that its owner was a glamour girl with whom he was currently sleeping. I had an idea if you asked him about it he would have given you a blueprint of her bedroom with her in it.

"This is my New York writer friend," Lanny said. He told him my name.

Hurd Evans glowed with correspondence school personality. He pumped my hand warmly, grinning from ear to ear. "I caught the road show of your play," he said. "It was a darb!"

"Thanks," I said.

But I didn't like him. He was scrubbed so clean you could smell the Lifebuoy. Lanny told him about the proposition, and I kept still. Lanny sat on the corner of his desk and waxed with extravagant eloquence. Finally he revealed that the Little Lady we had in mind was Vicky Lynn. Hurd Evans looked as though he had swallowed an avocado pit. His polished face reddened. He glanced at me.

"There's a fence around her," I said.

"Oh, sure." He laughed.

"Barbed wire," Lanny added. "The girl's as clean as a Johnson Office pamphlet to producers."

Hurd didn't believe this, and if he had he probably wouldn't have been interested; because Vicky would have had neither the oomph nor the heart for the hard fight that was ahead of us. But he only nodded.

"She's a fine girl," he said.

You would have thought from his tone that we intended billing her as an evangelist.

"So how about it?" asked Lanny. "It may mean putting up coin, you know."

"Hell, I've got a nickel saved," Hurd replied.

"Oke. You're in."

"Right."

"If it turns out good you get the glory for having 'discovered' her," Lanny said.

We all shook on it, and then the three of us went over to

18

the commissary for lunch. It was a low, long white building with a bulletin board of the studio's latest publicity clippings posted in front. Bing Crosby, in make-up, sat on the front steps exchanging chit-chat with messenger boys. Bing's bike was propped against the building. He rode it all over the lot whenever he was working. Actresses were going inside, wearing evening gowns, hula costumes, and one group, from the Old New York set, were garbed in clothes of the Gay Nineties.

There was a smaller commissary adjoining this one where the props, electricians, messengers and like company ate. But this main dining room was called the European Room, and it had no windows. It was designed on the order of the salon on the old *Queen Mary,* with murals on the wall, and music playing softly through a loud speaker. It was kept cool by air conditioning, and the tables were all crowded. The people sitting at them were laughing and talking.

At one long table there were two producers, their directors and assistants from one unit. At another sat a famous director-producer with his two male and one dowdy female writer and his associate director, mixing vitamins with story lines. Legitimate stars were scattered throughout the room and you could recognize more than a dozen familiar box-office faces. But what seemed to pack the place were the dress extras in costume who got twenty-five dollars a day and worked maybe one day a month. For them this was a show. It was like opening night at the opera. From the stately character actors to the torn-shirt-Elia Kazan-technique juveniles they sat regally in all their splendid dark make-up, Kleenex tissues tucked under their collars so the brown powder wouldn't smear. The women were radiant and elegant; some of them looked ravishing. On the street you wouldn't have looked twice at them, but now they were at their painted finest. They sat like bitchy little queens hoping that some agent who dropped in might notice they were working.

We stood waiting for the hostess to show us where to sit, and I noticed that throughout the room there was a lot of table to table visiting. Desperate, pitiful games were being played. "Well, old Horace, haven't seen you since *Ben*

Hur!" It had evidently been a hell of a time since Horace last worked. At a small table next to the wall near the place where waitresses stacked dirty dishes sat a director who had three weeks to go, but whose option was being dropped. He sat there like a ghost, nibbling at salad. No one wanted any part of him. No one could afford to be seen sitting with failure.

Lanny, Hurd and I were shown to a table. On the way I brushed against Rhonda Fleming's shoulder and smiled at her timidly. Then I ran smack into Marlon Brando. It was a lovely day! I heard two female extras arguing about who would pay the check. At the table I lit a cigarette.

"Don't ever be seen eating alone," Lanny said. "People'll think your option is being dropped."

I grabbed his sleeve and was nodding toward the door.

"All right," he said, "so it's Audrey Hepburn, what do you want me to do?"

It struck me then, all at once, that this world which glittered was the world into which I arrogantly imagined I could help catapult Vicky. It was suddenly very real. I was losing my courage. But Lanny Craig and Hurd Evans were talking about it with more enthusiasm than ever.

We had just finished soup when Robin Ray walked up. He had just come in from the Old New York set and hadn't found a table. He was afraid he might have to sit alone.

Robin Ray was a young juvenile. If you've ever seen him on the screen you probably forgot it an hour later. He doesn't make much impression. He's never played a lead and never will. Producers didn't decide that: it was the post cards they hand out to fans at previews. Stars are not made, they are elected. On the preview post card you vote for the actors who please you. You rate them. The actor himself never sees them, never knows. If his option is dropped he thinks it's studio politics.

Robin Ray had been in Hollywood one year and he had been in four pictures. His inter-studio rating was low, but he had a good publicity agent on the outside and for some reason the local papers thought he was good copy. You couldn't pick up *Daily Variety* or *The Reporter* without seeing him plugged in one column or another; and the Los Angeles theatrical pages were always crediting this brilliant new juvenile with sage quips his press agent copied out of Joe Miller Jokebooks. Of course the studio publicity department didn't like it. Nationally Robin got almost no publicity but locally he grabbed more space than the stars. It's the trade and local city papers that producers read. But the publicity department's bitter complaints that Robin's contract disallowed outside build-up was to no avail. His name appeared almost as often as that of Jack Paar.

"Gentlemen," he addressed us with actor's intonation, "gentlemen!"

"Don't insult us," said Lanny.

Robin laughed. Last night he had attended a première with the biggest star in the business and he felt pretty good. He confessed that he was all alone and asked if he could sit with us. Hurd Evans told him sure, park it. Robin pulled up a chair. That was how he happened to climb on Vicky's bandwagon.

"We've got a scheme," Lanny said. "You're just the boy we need."

We four sat around a table and made Vicky a star. Immediately after lunch we'd interview her and she'd sign a paper putting herself under our personal management for the next five years. She would have to have a talent agent to sell her to the studios but he would get only five percent of her salary instead of the usual ten. That was fair. We would collect the other five percent for our investment. Eventually there would be a profit since we also collected three percent as managers. That was eight altogether. The law won't let you take more than thirteen percent of any actor's pay. Our own actual outlay (besides our *time*) wouldn't be so much. The main item would be two hundred and fifty a month for a publicity agent. If she needed clothes for special occasions she could rent them from a wardrobe company. Almost everything else could be chiseled by pulling one string and another.

"This is a sweetheart," Hurd Evans said. "Once it starts it'll gather momentum. People'll think she's an angel dropped out of heaven."

It was decided that I'd take her to the highest priced flack

21

in town late that afternoon and get things started. Lanny and I would help the guy cook up stories. Her name would be linked romantically with Robin Ray. I protested, but they said a writer didn't have enough glamour and anyway, Robin was safe. They said Robin would take her to any big function where they'd be seen and get their pictures taken. Laughter and champagne copy. Robin's press agent would work on this angle so we'd really have two flacks busy turning out printed glamour for her. Meanwhile, Lanny would call up the West Coast editor of a picture magazine and talk him into a two-page spread on the Hollywood Cinderella angle. For this favor Lanny would get drunk with the editor and give him many lush telephone numbers. Hurd Evans would get in touch with a cosmetic company and Vicky'd do a series of pictures from a demure ingénue into a glamour girl. The process of being made up, step by step. Before and after. These would go in beauty magazines and drug store windows. I would phone my artist friend and persuade him to use her for a model on a magazine cover and then I'd write a brief article to tie up with it. Robin Ray would arrange that a certain radio columnist give her a send-off as a "sparkling comer."

We sat in the commissary until two-thirty and planned a background for her. That none of it was true made no difference. She was half French. Her father was a naval officer. She had been a débutante at swank Coronado. But, like other society creatures, she had been a blues singer with a band. The band had been playing Glendale when Hurd Evans had spotted her and rushed her to an agent on the Sunset Strip. And now she was on her way. Amen.

"It's like creating our own Cinderella," said Robin Ray. "Gentlemen, this thing fascinates me!"

Robin Ray was good looking and jovial, but you didn't quite trust him. Certainly he tried hard to be a regular guy. He was a little hurt that he wasn't always considered one. There had been a nasty crack in the trade papers that he couldn't keep one woman more than two weeks. This was his sore point. Once a rumor gets started about an actor it can finish him.

He wore a checked suit and a Kleenex tissue in his collar.

He smoked a cigarette. There was a heavy silver ring on his finger.

"I'm glad I got in on this," he said.

I asked him how *he* had gotten started.

"Well, you'll laugh." His voice was deep. "It was in the Little Theatre. *Straw Hat*. Somebody saw me."

Hurd Evans glanced at his watch. "Let's go see our merchandise," he said.

The four of us were in Hurd Evans' office when Vicky entered. She closed the door and stood there. She froze. She looks awful, I thought. We had been talking about her for hours. Nobody could have been so terrific as the girl we had been discussing. For a minute nobody spoke. Vicky thought maybe she was fired. She knew everyone by sight but I went through introductions.

"I'm charmed," said Robin Ray, "charmed. I understand we're going to hold hands in Winchell's column."

Vicky did a take-em. It was natural and she looked cute. We all sighed. We were started. The ice was broken.

"Let's see your legs," said Hurd Evans.

She glanced at me and I said no. Hurd Evans looked at me as though to say he supposed I could vouch for them. But it was all right. We called in a secretary. We dictated a letter to the studio for Vicky to sign saying that she was quitting. Then we made up a temporary contract. We'd give her money to live on if she needed it and pay for everything else. Vicky was shaking by now. She had gone white. She kept looking at me. She signed her name to everything in a jerky scrawl. Then she went to the door. She tried to thank us but her voice broke and she rushed into the hall.

"She's nice," Lanny Craig said, "nice!"

Vicky went home for the afternoon to get fixed up. When I picked her up at six o'clock she had taken a shower and changed clothes and she was fresh and pretty. I took her to Beverly Hills to see the press agent. We'd already talked turkey to him on the telephone.

This flack's name was Johnny Wismer. He was pretty big. They said if he took a girl on she couldn't miss. He was a thin, anaemic, sleepy-looking guy. His clothes were loose and just hung on him. He didn't get excited. He didn't smile or frown. He took down all the facts and some of the angles we had planned and kept saying, "Yeah . . . Yeah." In about two hours Vicky went out and I stayed there a minute.

"Well?"

"I'll take her on," he said. "That's my business. But she ain't got a prayer."

I went cold.

"I'll give you two to one any day in the week she'll never top Jayne Mansfield."

"Well," I said, "even if she doesn't—"

He stuck a cigarette in his mouth and grinned. "Yeah. Even if she doesn't, that ain't hay, is it?"

"No," I said, "it ain't hay." We shook hands and I went out.

I never knew what glamour could do. You'd think I'd have had sense and realize it was all faked. But no. Vicky was confused and scared more than happy. But I regarded her differently. I couldn't believe she was quite real. There is the story of the press agent who built up a girl, then fell in love with the glamour he'd made. It was going to be like that. I could feel it already.

Jill was at the apartment and she ate dinner with us in the kitchenette. The band had broken up. Jill just listened to everything we told her and she seemed to be transfixed. Her hair was copper under the electric light and her eyes were very blue. She thought it was wonderful. She wasn't a bit jealous. She wore a yellow house dress and a white apron. She cooked the dinner. But when it was all on the table, Vicky couldn't eat. She said she would be all right. She just wanted to go in the bedroom and cry a little.

I sat opposite Jill at the table. My head was singing. Jill ate her food and watched. Then she stopped eating and wiped her pretty mouth with a napkin.

"You're swell, Peg."

"But this is going to be fun," I said.

"I don't care. You're swell."

After a while Vicky came out and had coffee with us. In

about an hour Lanny Craig came over. He gave Vicky a fatherly kiss and then he shook both of Jill's hands. He walked with a limp to the divan and sat down and made a place for Jill.

Hurd Evans arrived next. The little guy wore a tuxedo. He still looked dandy. Lanny had told me that he had a rotten temper. He had been known to slap a woman in public. He looked *so* bright and gay I could believe it! He was still Joe College to me. If he'd told a girl in the sticks that he was a director she would have laughed at him. He came in and kissed Vicky behind the ears. He treated her like a goddess. That's the way we all felt. Then he sat down and made a bid for Jill. But he was very friendly about it. He and Lanny were old pals.

"Don't let mama catch you out, Lanny, or she'll be in Reno tomorrow."

"Mama doesn't make me wear a slave bracelet," Lanny said.

Hurd Evans looked at the bracelet. "A very dear friend gave me that," he said solemnly.

We all laughed and the bell rang and it was Robin Ray. He made the magnificent entrance. He was lit. He wore tails, white tie, and a top hat. He strode in dramatically, pulling something on a piece of string behind him. He took off his top hat with a wide sweep and bowed low, first to Vicky, whose finger tips he kissed, and then to Jill. Then he turned around and hauled in on the string. Tied to it was a caravan of three cardboard boxes; the first was loaded with bottles of Scotch and the second two were heaped with roses. There were five dozen of them. Red and yellow and white. We had just emptied the boxes when the bell rang again. Robin answered it and his chauffeur came in, carrying a case of imported champagne packed in ice. He put it in the kitchen, and departed without a word. There were flowers and bottles of Scotch all over the floor and Robin stood among them, bowing again, to Vicky, then to Jill. He was smiling, a broad smile. Then he put on his hat and took Vicky in his arms and kissed her on the lips.

"You're my girl," he said, "for keeps."

"But—"

"In the newsprints, sweet. In cold black type . . . but alas, not in the flesh! With bitter envy I am compelled to bow to the gentleman on my right." He bowed to me. "You have my solemn word that I'll make no passes—while he's in the room."

Lanny Craig laughed. Hurd and Jill started gathering the flowers. We had to send downstairs for more vases and glasses. Harry Williams left the switchboard to bring them up. When he saw the littered room his white face looked puzzled. His yellow eyes blinked behind the thick lens of his glasses. He scowled at me. Robin Ray spotted him. He strode over and kissed Harry on either cheek.

"You may exit, Jasper," he said.

Harry was stunned, confused. He stared at Robin.

"Dr. Cyclops," Robin said. "Be gone, dog!"

Harry Williams moved toward the door. He turned back once. We were all looking at him. I think he would have said something nasty but he was afraid of being fired. He went out, slamming the door.

"Just a sweetheart," Hurd Evans said.

"Yes, isn't he?"

"Don't ever get trapped in a broken elevator with him, Jill," Lanny said.

After that we forgot him, and the party got hilarious. It was the beginning of something: an epoch. Vicky was never more beautiful. But I noticed she didn't pay so much attention to me now. It was Robin's show and I guess he dazzled her. Hell, he dazzled me! He was an exhibitionist—but he was really funny. I thought it was a shame they made him play straight in the films. Robin said that champagne and Scotch mixed was the best drink in seven countries. He said it was known as the drink of the Hollywood Virgin. He gave Vicky the first glass, then he mixed the others. It was a fine party. I guess I couldn't blame Vicky for leaving me alone so much. Only, even with all the noise and the music and the drinking, I felt a stab of loneliness. It was Jill who came to me.

"What's the matter, Peg?"

"Nothing," I said.

"Vicky really appreciates you doing all this for her."

26

"Sure," I said, "I know."

I remember at midnight we stood Vicky up on the kitchenette table and drank to her, and she said this was the happiest moment in her life. She stood up there and said: "I love you all very dearly."

Chapter Four

We were all crazy the next few weeks. History was made in Hollywood. A magic legend was created and her name was Vicky Lynn. In the movies they call it montage. Gaudy and noisy. Scenes, and bits of music; snatches of dialogue, and laughter; the flash of cameras, the clatter of typewriters. All of it building . . . building . . . building. These are the things I remember:

Hurd Evans: "Yes, I discovered her. She was singing with a band in Glendale. . . ."

Vicky: "It was Mr. Evans who saw me first. It was at a navy party in Coronado."

The flack: "Hell, no, she was never a secretary. Who ever said she was a secretary? She never saw a typewriter in her life!"

Robin Ray: "When I saw her I knew she'd be the girl. It'll be Vicky and me from now on. No, we haven't set a date. Her career, you see—"

Lanny Craig: "Sure, we're sponsoring her. Who wouldn't sponsor her if they had the chance?"

Jill: "You're swell, Peg. You're real."

Vicky: "Baby, I love you. Don't be jealous of Robin. I love *you!* There's nothing I wouldn't do for you. Here, I want you to have the key to my apartment. If I have to go out to a première, you go in and wait for me. No, keep the key. I'll have another made. Kiss me, baby. Are my tears wet, darling? You're wonderful, have I told you?"

Pictures with make-up on. Pictures with make-up off. Vicky sitting still and one of the country's best artists painting her for a magazine. Vicky sitting in the Sunset Strip office of Max Epstein, the talent agent. Listening to him as he talks, slowly and carefully, choosing one word after another. When you go in to interview a man look at him as though he were the only man in the world. Make it seem as though you are breathless. We are selling the charm of your youth. We are selling your sex.

Portraits of Vicky for the studios. Leg art. Bathing suits and rented formals. Portraits laughing. Portraits of tragedy. Vicky walking up and down the apartment with books on her head. Vicky learning how to make up with grease paint. Vicky, gorgeous and radiant, with grace, with poise, with natural ease.

Vicky at a première. The floodlights shining down on her, the crowds surging behind ropes. Vicky coming in, splendid in a silver gown, on the arm of Robin Ray. Robin in tails, smiling and beaming. Flashlight pictures. A word in the radio microphone. Lovely Vicky Lynn, Hollywood's newest personality.

These are the things publicity buys!

Vicky Lynn, black type, Hollywood columns . . . *Vicky Lynn*, syndicate ticker tape . . . *Vicky Lynn*, trade papers . . . *Vicky Lynn*, her first fan magazine break.

Lunch at the Brown Derby with Robin. Vicky being pushed through dramatic school. Open your mouth wide. Now say *Ah. Ah . . . ah . . . ah.* Put these stones in your mouth and talk. Scream, please. Cry, please, your heart is broken, cry. No, not that way!

Hurd Evans, his coat off, walking up and down in his shirt sleeves, sweating. Lanny Craig watching. Hurd: "No, Vicky, you'd come in a scene like this. You don't give a damn, see? You pretend there isn't any camera. It isn't the stage. They can always shoot it again . . ."

Midnight lights. Dancing lessons. Singing instruction. Vicky in blue tights and a white jacket, tap dancing, worn out, but laughing. Vicky in Romanoff's with Robin. At the Grove with Robin. At Dave Chasen's with Robin.

Vicky: "Baby, you and I *can't* be seen anywhere, don't you see? If they thought this romance was a press build-up —they're so sick of phony romances, and so suspicious!"

Vicky: "No, baby. I didn't kiss him. Except good-night. I kissed him good-night. That's why my lipstick is smeared.

I think he's lovely, baby. But he's not for me!"

Vicky: "Johnny Wismer says my press notices are ripe now and next week Max Epstein's taking me around for studio interviews. Three studios have already called. They want to see me!"

Vicky: "Baby, tomorrow I get a screen test. *A screen test!*"

I remember the night before the screen test. Everything was very quiet. It was the lull before the stardom. Vicky was different. She had all the glamour in the world. Four tired guys had worked day and night. They had hired the best flacks in the world. They had secured the best talent agent on the Sunset Strip. Everybody had worked. And now Vicky was a personality. She shone like the sun. She was beautiful like the moon. She was bright like the stars. I went up to her apartment and used the key she had given me and went in. I had been in and out so much I didn't knock any more. She and Jill were there, sitting there. I still had on slacks and a sports jacket.

I said: "Vicky, cook us some dinner."

She stared at me. Tomorrow she might never have to cook a dinner again. But I saw that she was pouting. I was kidding her, and she'd grown angry.

So Jill and I started dinner. Vicky got feeling sheepish and came out and volunteered to help. But we wouldn't let her. We treated her like Miss Rich Bitch, pulling back her chair at the table and helping her into it. But before the meal was over we'd laughed it off. I said I'd gotten my story treatment okayed and had somehow managed to finish the first rough draft of my screen play. I said I didn't know how I'd done it, but it wasn't bad.

After dinner we went for a drive. We took Jill. I drove down Wilshire to the beach. We saw the lawns and the still palms and the stars gaudy in the sky. It was October, and warm, an Indian summer, and I thought of Victor Herbert's beautiful song. I was glad all the clamor of the build-up was over.

"If the screen test gets you a contract, you won't have to see Robin any more, will you?" I said.

"Oh, it wouldn't be right to break off so quickly." She was sulky.

29

"No, I guess it—it wouldn't be right." I looked over at Jill. "Will you sing, Jill? It's so quiet it would be nice."

Jill sang. Her voice was soft and rich. She had gotten a job singing fifteen minute spots on the radio. But this was different and better. Pretty soon we were all singing, very softly, and we drove along the Palisades, and down past the beach, the waves crashing on the sand, and the moon running across the water. We sang and we didn't talk any more. But when we were driving back to town Vicky said:

"Haven't you noticed, baby? Jill's in love with you."

It was as though someone had hit Jill.

"Don't be silly, Vicky," I said. "You're being childish."

"No, really. I've known for a long time. She's tried to cover it up. But I've known."

"You're jealous," I said "and silly. Besides, I don't love Jill. I don't love her at all."

The silence was terrible. Jill just sat there and didn't say anything. She tried to hum but she couldn't. We were all very quiet, and the car seemed empty and dark, and the stars were white and naked, and there was no breeze in the palms at all.

The next day it rained and I wore my old gray suit to the studio. I didn't wear that suit much any more—but today it felt good. Nothing was right. I sat and watched the rain. A block or so away Vicky was in another studio. She was on a sound stage. The cameras would be ready. They'd put a male stock player with her. Lanny Craig would be there and Hurd Evans to coach her if they'd let him, and Robin Ray would be there. Vicky wouldn't be nervous. She was too well trained to be nervous now. She was smooth and polished. That studio was getting a break! I was tortured. I kept remembering last night. I was a little crazy. I had a hundred moods one after another. One was rage. I sat at the desk and scrawled a note to Vicky. I said that if she loved Robin I'd want to kill her. I said that she was my day and night obsession, that there wasn't anything without her. But it was no good. I balled up the note and jammed it in my pocket. I tried typing her a gay little letter with a bitter undertone. But that didn't come off, either. I walked around the office. I had turned in my script and it wasn't likely the producer would call me on it today. I decided to go to my hotel. I left and stopped at a bar on the way. I got to the hotel late that night and slept and didn't wake up until it was morning.

Vicky called then. "Baby, it was okay! I sign the contract in Max Epstein's office at two o'clock this afternoon."

"How much?"

"Well, there're rising options, seven years of—"

"I know all about options."

"Three hundred a week to start."

"Swell," I said, "you're on your way now, kid!" I tried to hold my voice up. But it sagged all over the place. It'd be Vicky and Robin now. Goodbye, I thought. I wish to hell you were a secretary again.

"Honey, I've got *so* many things to do—meet me at the apartment at four."

"All right. Gee, I'm happy for you, kid!"

She was excited on the phone. "I love you, baby," she said.

I got to the apartment at six o'clock and used the key and went in. I remember it was quiet. Then I saw her. She was lying on the floor, one arm stretched out. She wore a light afternoon dress and her figure was beautiful. She was as white as marble but she looked lovely. Her hair was splayed out in fine strands of gold, and her lips were bright, rich red, and there was a green eye-shadow on her eyelids. You could see that because her eyes were closed and she was lying very still. She was lying still and she wasn't breathing.

Chapter Five

I didn't feel anything. I moved slowly and numbly across the room, and I stood there, and then I knelt down, empty and trembling, my eyes dry and vacant. She was lovely. Christ, she was exquisite. I saw that somebody had hit her just behind the ear. I leaned forward. I kissed her on the lips.

She was cold!

I touched both of her shoulders.

Dead. Dead! *Dead!*

It was like I'd gone crazy. Everything was turmoil. I began to talk to her. We could have had such fun, Vicky and me!

"Who did it, Vicky? What dirty son of a bitch did this? I'll live until I tear the bleeding guts out of the killer!"

I began choking. I heard somebody at the door. What the hell did I care? I heard a key in the lock. I didn't give a damn! All I wanted to do was run away with Vicky. I wanted to run over the roof tops with her and look down and laugh at all the bastards on an earth where there wasn't any Vicky! I wanted to—

"Peg!"

I straightened up. My back was stiff and full of electricity. My back was like the back of a cat. I sat there on my legs and didn't move. I heard Jill coming across the room. But it was a room somewhere else. It was a hollow room made of metal. I heard her footsteps. I heard her scream. She screamed again and I heard the echo. She was down on her knees. She was shaking Vicky. I crawled away. I didn't get up; I crawled away. I crawled up to a chair and hung on to it and put my head in my arms.

A long time passed. Ten years passed. I heard Jill breathing. The room was quiet. It was quiet and dark. The windows off the fire escape were open and the wind was cold. The night was cold. Traffic swished by on Franklin Avenue. I heard Jill move. I heard her voice. I couldn't see her.

"You killed her!"

I didn't say anything. I sat there not crying and my heart beating and my head hot and cheeks hot and I didn't say anything.

"You killed her!"

(We toasted her with champagne. We all stood there and toasted her, and Vicky was on the kitchenette table, and she said this was the happiest moment in all her life . . .)

"Peg, I'm going to kill you."

(She looked up tenderly and she said, That's funny, nobody ever bought me a white orchid before!)

"Do you hear me?"

"Yes—yes, and do you think for Christ's sake that I—I could—" My voice choked off.

Jill was standing over me now. She was there and I could see the outline of her face in the light from the street. Then she was down beside me, pulling on my arm and crying. She was full of misery and pain and she was crying.

"Forgive me for even thinking it! Will you forgive me, Peg! I knew Vicky so well! I loved her so much! Can you *ever* forgive me!"

I could still hear the traffic, and now a night bird, a California night bird.

"Listen, Jill. Listen," I said, "stay away from me. Just stay the hell away! I don't want anybody around. I don't want—will you take your hands off me!"

My face came up, bright and wet and hard, and I could see in the darkness. Jill took her hands away and sat on her legs, sobbing. We sat motionless and silent and the sodden sounds from the street crept up to us on an echo and chattered with the tick of the kitchen clock.

"You'd better call the cops," I said.

The light was bright and hot and my eyes burned and there was sweat on my face and my tongue was thick and heavy. They kept smoking cigarettes and talking. They kept talking. I tried to make answers but my lips were parched and stuck together. I was thirsty and they picked up a spittoon and washed my face with the water in it. The water and the tobacco juice. I licked my lips with my dry tongue. I tried to see but I couldn't. That light was like the sun. It was like the desert and the sun. Now they jerked me to my feet and took me out into the hall. The pupils of my eyes were dilating but I still couldn't see anything. Somebody hit me. He smacked me right across the mouth. I felt the blood hot in between my teeth and I tried to suck it out and drink it. They hit me again. It felt like my jaw was broken. They hit me with fists. They took hold of my hair and bounced my head against the wall. They shook me up. They pulled me away

33

from the wall and knocked me down. They picked me up and knocked me down again. I could feel the pain and the rising welts. All of my teeth were aching. That was the worst. All of my teeth kept aching at once. I had a mouth full of ache. My tongue was cut. My eyes were swollen. They knocked me down again and jerked me up. Some guy held me by the front of my shirt. My brown sports shirt. He pushed me backwards into the same room with the light. I choked on the smoke. I was bleeding like hell. They sat me down.

"You're going to hang, mister."

"Then for Christ's sake hang me."

"Make it easy on yourself. You'll hang anyway. Why'd you kill her?"

"I didn't kill her."

"You didn't mean to, did you? You didn't mean to, we know that."

"That's fine," I said.

"Then you admit it?"

"No." I spit up a mouthful of blood. It drooled over my chin, and it was thick and hot in my mouth, and I could scarcely get the words out, and I don't know how they understood me, the thick, wet, blubbered words, but they did.

"Tell us everything. Tell us what you did all day."

"I—have. I've—told you."

"Tell us again, mister. Sing it this time, hot shot. Ain't you a pretty sight! Tell us again. Go on, tell us!"

"I woke. She telephoned. Prom—promised to see her—four o'clock. I started to go to work but I didn't. I didn't feel like it."

"You didn't feel like it because you thought she was in love with this actor. This Robin Ray."

"Maybe."

"Put that down. He was jealous of this actor. You didn't know who else she was playing around with, either, did you?"

"*Shuddup.*"

"Go on. You didn't go to work. Where did you go?"

"I walked. I walked out Sunset and took a bus back."

"What time was it then?"

"I don't know. I had lunch. A malted milk with two eggs in it and a bacon and tomato sandwich . . . After that I went to the newsreel theatre on Hollywood Boulevard. I felt lousy and I wanted to kill time. The newsreel was about missiles and rockets. There was a reel about bathing beauties. There was a reel about fashion."

"Never mind."

"I came out. I didn't know what time it was."

"It didn't occur to you to look? You had a date with the woman you loved. But it didn't occur to you to look and see what time it was?"

I couldn't see this guy that was talking but I felt him and I knew him. I knew him inside and out. I knew his name and all about him. In the hours these things had come to me. His name was Ed Cornell and he was a homicide detective. He was about thirty. He had red hair and thin white skin and red eyebrows and blue eyes. He looked sick. He looked like a corpse. His clothes didn't fit him. He wore a derby. Nobody in California wears a derby but Ed Cornell wore one. He was a misfit. But the rest of them thought he was smart. He was frail, gray-faced and bitter. He was possessed with a macabre humor. His voice was nasal. You'd think he was crying. He might have had T.B. He looked like he couldn't stand up in a wind. He was thin and his face was gaunt. He kept lighting cigarettes and flicking the lit matches in my face.

I said: "I didn't know what time it was because I didn't know if I would go and see her. When I first met her she wouldn't give me a tumble until I pretended indifference. I thought I would see what she would do if I didn't show up."

"So you went to a bar."

"I went to a bar."

"You went to a bar on Hollywood Boulevard," said Ed Cornell, "but the waiter doesn't even remember seeing you."

"Doesn't he?"

"No. He doesn't remember. We called him."

"Well, it was a dark bar, and it was crowded, and I sat back in a corner."

"Then what did you do?"

"I thought."

"What did you think?"

"I thought today Vicky would be very happy and it would be a lousy trick for me not to show up and congratulate her."

"In other words, you changed your mind?"

"Yes."

"You decided you wouldn't be indifferent, after all?"

"That's what I decided."

"You didn't wait for her outside of her agent's office on Sunset and pick her up at, say—three-thirty?"

"No."

"You didn't pick her up and take her to her apartment and kill her?"

"No."

"Listen, mister. Some of the fur of her silver fox jacket was on the blue upholstery in the front seat of your car."

"It got there yesterday."

"You said you didn't see her yesterday."

"Then it was the day before."

"Did you ever argue with her about Robin Ray?"

"Yes, plenty."

"Did you ever threaten her?"

"No."

"Did you ask her to stop seeing him?"

"Yes."

"What did you hit her with this afternoon?"

I tried to look at him but I couldn't see anything. "Why don't you change the needle," I said. He slapped me. He picked up my hand and put out the lighted end of his cigarette in the palm of it. I didn't move.

"How much did you give Harry Williams?" he said.

"Who's Harry Williams?"

"You don't know him?"

"No."

"Put that down." To me: "Harry Williams worked on the switchboard in the apartment house."

"Oh, him."

"What do you know about him?"

"Nothing. He was a dope."

"You don't know anything else?"

"He had a crush on Vicky."

"You say that."

"Ask her sister," I said.

"Why don't you talk, mister?"

I didn't say anything.

"You're smooth but I know personally that you killed her. I don't care what the rest of them think; I know what I know. I've never been wrong in my life. I've never failed to bring in a conviction. Sometimes it took me five or six years but I never fail. I live alone in a hotel room in Los Angeles. I stay there and think about these cases. I'm not married and I don't chase. And I'm going to hang you, mister. Now or later I'm going to hang you. I'm going to build up an air-tight case. I'm going to build up a jury proof case and hang you. I know how to do it. I have ways. Sometimes they aren't nice ways. But they always look fine in court. I work when I'm off duty. I never stop working. One day I'll die in bed and I'll still be working. You're such a smooth baby. But you'll see. Ed Cornell will put a noose around your stinking neck. Open your eyes and listen to me! You'll never get away. As long as you live you'll never get away!"

I keeled over.

I woke up in the cell. It was damp and cold and some guys were shaking me. All of my teeth ached. I told them to stop shaking me. It was cold and the fog was coming in. The floor felt wet. My teeth kept aching. Somebody gave me a cigarette. They lit it for me and I puffed and inhaled. There were about four guys in the room and I thought they were going to beat me again. But they just stood around and waited for me to smoke a little. Then they gave me a drink of water and helped me to my feet. They took me down a long corridor and I saw cells on either side. They took me out some kind of a back exit and put me in a sedan. I was chattering with cold. My teeth kept aching.

They drove me through the streets very fast and nobody said anything. There were three of us in the back, me in the middle. When I wanted another cigarette they gave it to me. I couldn't see where we were. We turned a lot of corners and we might have been going around and around the block. I won't say we were but that's the way it seemed. But after a while we went straight. We went straight for miles and then I saw Hollywood Boulevard. It was about four in the morning. They stopped the car at an all night drug store and took me in.

The pharmacist didn't say anything either. He didn't say yes or no or go to hell. He looked at me and then he went and got some adhesive and some iodine and other stuff and fixed me up. He worked on me for a long time. I tried to tell him my teeth ached but I was chattering.

They put me back in the car and drove about two blocks and stopped again at a barbecue stand. A girl came out to the car. She looked very tired. She said, "Hello, Gus," to one of the men. They ordered food for me. Soft eggs and coffee. I sat there in the middle in the back of the car and ate it. It tasted very good except that my teeth kept aching. Once one of the men flicked on a radio and I heard part of a police call and then he flicked the radio off again. Those two men in the front and the two in the back sat there smoking and waiting for me. Before we left they let me get out and took me around behind the barbecue stand and waited for me until I came out.

Then we were all in the car again and drove some more. It was getting light. It was a tarnished nickel dawn and it was cracking holes in the sky. I could see tall palms blocked against it. I knew where we were going now. We were on Seventh Avenue and going down into Los Angeles. They stopped the car in front of the city jail and I had the queer feeling that this was where we had started from. But of course I was wrong. I know I was wrong. They all said so. I couldn't be right about that. I couldn't say anything for sure. I don't know where I'd been the night before. These guys were all very nice to me. They joked viciously about Ed Cornell. They called me pal and asked me if I had the phone numbers of any movie stars. They asked me how my ribs felt and I said my ribs felt all right but my teeth ached. They took me into the building. We walked down halls and went up in an elevator. I think we were in some sort of a police barracks. I'm not sure. They didn't say. But there was a room with a bed in it. The sheets weren't clean but it was all right. They told me to lie down with my clothes on and take it easy. I lay down and went to sleep.

The assistant D. A.'s office was bright and sunny. He sat across from me in a swivel chair. He was tapping a pencil on the desk blotter and he looked upset.

"There's been a terrible mistake," he said.

I didn't say anything.

He got ingratiating. "You look a mess!" He smiled. "Do you know where you were last night?"

"No."

"It wasn't Los Angeles or Hollywood," he said.

"No?"

"No. You were taken to a little nearby town." He paused. "Do you want to know what town it was?"

"It doesn't matter."

He looked relieved. "Are you—interested in the names of the men who—who questioned you last night?"

"No."

"I see. That's sensible. Of course, they made a terrible mistake and they'll answer for it. I can assure you that at least two of them will be demoted because of it."

"It makes no difference to me," I said.

"My, that's very generous of you," he said sarcastically. "It was just that the boys felt sure at first that you were guilty of Miss Lynn's murder and they were trying to break you down." He paused. "You shouldn't blame them if—"

"No, I don't blame them."

"It won't do you any good to be bitter," he said.

"Oh, for Christ's sake!" I said. "I won't raise a stink, if that's what's worrying you!"

"It isn't. Don't worry. It didn't happen in my jurisdiction. We don't work that way in Los Angeles."

"No," I said, "naturally." My eyes were hot.

"It seemed logical that you were the guilty one."

"Doesn't it now?" I watched him. I held my breath and watched him.

He put down the pencil and folded his hands. "No," he said. "We think we know the identity of the killer."

"You—you know?"

He was back like a cat. "Is it so unusual we should know?"

I eased off. "Who is it?"

"A man named Harry Williams, we believe. He's missing. He's been missing since five-thirty last night. He was around the apartment until then."

"Harry Williams!"

"Yes. It's our theory that he saw Miss Lynn when she came in. We have it on your word and the word of her sister that he was infatuated with Vicky Lynn. We believe he followed her up to the apartment and on some pretext entered. Of course, he had the pass key at his disposal and that wouldn't have been very hard."

"You think it's a sex crime?"

"Yes."

"She wasn't raped?"

"No. We work it out in this way. He tried to embrace Miss Lynn and she fought him. He was a stupid and slow-thinking man and in his rage he picked up something and hit her with it. The coroner tells us that she was hit by something much harder than just a fist. Whatever this object was, Williams must have taken it with him. We can't find it now.

"After he hit her he regained his senses. He stared down at her, filled with terror. His previous intentions were gone. He knew he had to lam—and he did. Didn't even stop by his room for clothes. And he's probably holed up somewhere in town—scared and shaky. We put out dodgers on him. He's being word-mugged on teletype all along the line—all state and local gendarmes. The little rat hasn't a chance!"

"I'm glad. Christ, this all sounds so familiar—"

He nodded. "Murders run to form—just like anything else. This preyed on Williams' mind. When the publicity started he knew she'd be moving to a better apartment—that he'd lose all track of her—he got panicky—"

"I'd like to get my hands on him," I said, "just once!"

40

I remember that the fresh earth beside the grave was brown and wet, and that the black coffin was shiny in the sun. I remember that I did not cry, but just stood there, even when the men with the spades went away, and then, after that, I do not remember at all the things I did that day.

Chapter Six

The town was hot, and it was dusty, and the palms were still; the air was stagnant and listless and the streets were empty but for lazy, slow-walking people who did nothing all day but walk, or sit on benches, or join pension groups, or feed the pigeons. This was Los Angeles. The pigeons were everywhere, strutting about, fat and greedy, and the pigeons liked this, but for us, the idle, the walkers, the hands-in-the-pockets desolates, every day was a separate world, every day was two hundred hours long, and only in the dusk when the buses roared by, filled with secretaries and stenographers from the downtown companies, did it seem to be a town, and then only for a little while; after that it was night and couples walked the streets, or lay in the grass in MacArthur Park watching the cars stream over the Wilshire bridge.

I walked through the day and through the night and I saw these things and heard them; and after a few days I went downtown and walked on Main Street with the bums, and here it was always the same, the moochers and the two-bit merchants, and the blondes that taxi-danced with Gooks; they kept moving all the time in a stream and they didn't look at you if you needed a shave, and you could get a breakfast with two eggs and bacon and coffee for ten cents. You saw burlesque shows and hock shops and the Army and Navy store; and down near the Plaza the gaudy red and green signs advertising movies in Spanish, and Mexicans and Indians standing around on street corners.

Down here there was an old mission, so old that if you

touched the 'dobe wall it crumbled under your fingers. It was always open but in the daytime it was deserted, and it was dark inside, the candles flickering beside the altar, throwing jagged shadows across the statues of Saints, reminding them of humble prayers. You could kneel down here on the wooden dieu, and it was very quiet, and sometimes you thought the old Padres were watching you.

But after that the daylight didn't seem quite real. Then you could go across from the Plaza to the cobblestone alley of Olvera Street, which is very Mexican and festive, and is kept up for tourists. It is only one short block but it is a whole country and you want to laugh. They try to sell you everything. You can buy a sombrero or a 'dobe Saint or a painted turtle; you can have your fortune told, or a paper silhouette made while you wait, or you can sit in a little café and listen to a Mexican string band. It is like Mexico in the daytime because there are no tourists. You can sleep on a doorstep and no one will bother you.

The little bar was here, on Olvera Street, and I sat in it, drinking. I sat up to the bar and there were two Mexicans at the other end, talking volubly, and behind me there were two more at a small table, playing cards. It was just a crumby little place and everyone was talking Spanish. I sat very still and didn't move except to lift my arm. Outside the daylight was gray and there were shadows and red streaks of fire in the sky, and pretty soon it would be dark. I pushed my whiskey pony forward again. The boy filled it up. I put two bits on the counter and he took it, and stuck it in the cash register.

I looked at myself in the mirror. It was a bad, unwashed mirror, and there was steam on it, and an uneven row of half-empty bottles lined up at the bottom of it. Then, suddenly, I saw *him*.

He was sitting beside me. It must have just happened. I didn't remember looking down or away but now here he was. At first I didn't believe it. I just thought I was looking at pain. But it breathed and I could see that I was wrong, it was Ed Cornell. He was wearing the derby and it was pushed back on his head. His sideburns were red and his

42

skin was thin and white and unhealthy. He asked for a glass of water, and kept watching me in the mirror.

"How'd you find me?" My voice was thick and low.

"I can find anybody," he said.

"Jesus! You've been *ten days* hunting me down!"

"The studio said you were on lay-off; you never appeared at the hotel. But we meet just the same, mister."

I was silent. He was like the ghost of my agony sitting there. My fingers trembled against the whiskey pony. I lifted it to drink and he spoke again.

"Doing this won't help you forget you killed her."

My hand jerked and I splashed the whiskey straight into his white face. He took out a handkerchief and wiped it away. He was unexcited: except for the light in his eyes. He looked like something embalmed by a medical student who'd done a bad job. He soured my guts.

"What's the matter," I said, "you yellow? I've heard something about you, I—"

"Shut your mouth and listen to me. Have you seen the papers?"

"For what?" I said. "The last thing I read was an obituary column and that fed me up. Shall I tell you about it?"

"Harry Williams hasn't been found," Ed Cornell went on.

"*You* can find *anybody*," I said.

"I can find anybody in town. A guy that gets paid like you do could get any man out of town very easily."

"I see. *I* got him out of town."

"Sure. He was around when you killed the girl. You paid him off. You threatened to kill him if he came back."

"Very sweet," I said. "That's very sweet."

"That's what I figured," said Ed Cornell.

"It's very sweet, and you're very specific."

"I have my own ideas."

"Another whiskey," I told the bartender. I looked over at Ed Cornell. "They didn't demote you in rank, did they?"

"They might have."

"You're a liar," I said. "You're a stinking, two-bit liar." I opened my hand and showed him the blisters his cigarettes had made, then I pushed the hand into his face. He rocked back. He grabbed my wrist. I said:

43

"Let go of me or I'll kill you."

He let go of me.

I drank my drink. "So the cops don't think Harry Williams killed her? They changed their minds."

"I don't give a damn what the cops think," Ed Cornell said.

"Oh. Oh, I see. *They* still believe Williams is guilty. You're the hold-out. You're the bright boy. Everybody's out of step except you."

"I'm off duty now. When I'm off duty I can think what I want. I hunted you down only during the hours I was off duty. I have my personal opinions. I've never been wrong yet."

"Never?"

"Never. I know types. They say sex crime. It's easy. It's off the books that way. But he isn't the type."

"There's no way of telling types," I said.

"Yes, there is. Not by the face. I never saw his face. I asked questions about him. I went through his room. He wouldn't have done it."

"Why?"

"What's the difference why? It happens I know. These things run to pattern. I've been through dozens of them. But there were no nude pictures in his room. No hot magazines or books. The guy was a vegetable. He bolted his door nights. He wouldn't have gone near her. Not him!"

"But you've no *physical* evidence that it wasn't he?"

"We have no physical evidence that it was. Are you worried about it? We don't need that."

"I see. I'm applauding dismal brilliance. But listen, Cornell. Have you ever been to a dentist?"

He didn't say anything.

"It's very nice," I said. "I spent three days with one last week." I was opening and closing my fist. He looked down at it.

"That won't do any good."

"Quit saying that!"

"It won't stop you from inhaling that gas when the pellet drops."

I shoved him back off the stool. I got up, swaying unsteadily. I bunched up the front of his coat and held him by it and cocked my fist. But I couldn't hit him. He was frail. He looked sick. I heard him wheezing for his breath. He began to cough. I had his coat up and I didn't see any gun holster. I pushed him back.

"Get out of here!"

The Mexicans had stopped talking and were looking at us. They didn't want any part of it. I had bumped the card table. Ed Cornell's voice was bitter. He was like a straw in the wind.

"*You* claim you loved Vicky Lynn!"

"*Shuddup!*"

His voice dripped with scorn. "You claim you loved her! But I tell you Harry Williams didn't kill her and it doesn't phase you. If you loved her you wouldn't want to rest 'til you'd found out who it was. But you don't. You sit here sopping up whiskey because your conscience is festering with big broken sores that hurt your guts!"

There was a terrible ring in what he said and I could suddenly see him walking through the streets looking for me, going from place to place, making telephone call after telephone call, with his own dimes, all the time his mind churning, churning, churning, like a hurdy-gurdy, rehearsing the things he was going to tell me, the essence of nothing, wrapped in macabre bitterness; the acid spew of a warped hatred, for it was not a murder he was prosecuting, but a personal obsession; this now was obvious. He hated me. For ten days and nights he had hunted me, and now he had me, I was found, but he could do nothing, and his tongue rattled with prepared words, while the real fury shrieked all through him and was soundless.

"I'll tell you something else. I'm not married. I don't chase."

"You said that that night."

"I stay in my room. I don't have a girl. I'm a sick man and I'm no good to any woman. But I can wish, see? I think how it must be. Sometimes I do. I wish about women. But none of them were ever worth it, and it didn't affect me much."

"What the hell do I care what affected you?" I said.

"But this one was worth it," he went on. "I found out. I've seen her parents. I've talked to everybody that knew her. Everybody, see? I know her history. I know her better than she ever knew herself. I've been living in her echo. I've got pictures of her . . . and some of her perfume. I've got a little lace handkerchief she used. And stockings and a brassière. I've got some of her letters, snapshots with writing on the back, and theater programs, and a telegram you sent her once when you couldn't take her to dinner. There was lipstick on it because she kissed it, and I guess she must have cried. I guess—"

"*Shuddup!*" I said. "I don't want to listen. The cops told me about you. You impotent bastard!"

He stopped on the word impotent. It was as though I'd hit him with my fist. He stared at me. His cheeks were blotchy red. The wind was gone out of him. For a moment it looked as though he wanted to crawl away. Now he sucked for his breath and his eyes came up. He seemed to be choking.

"Well, why don't you laugh? It's a big joke, isn't it? The impotent cop. Ain't that a funny thing? Impotent and about to die at thirty. Anybody could laugh, see? The way I sit in my room at night and cough and spit and look at the pretty pictures of Vicky Lynn."

I couldn't look at him. I was sorry for what I said. I didn't want to hurt *any* man the way Ed Cornell was hurt. He was talking.

"Pictures . . . all around the room. You see them wherever you look. A sickly guy who can only love a girl that's dead. Ain't that a laugh, mister? But, listen. In the end you won't laugh, and you won't push me around any more. You'll end up in the gas chamber and it'll be Vicky and I that'll laugh . . . that's exactly what we'll do, mister! We'll laugh at your stinking corpse!"

For a moment there was silence and then I heard a door slam. Ed Cornell was gone.

Chapter Seven

I returned to the studio on Monday. I arrived at a quarter of ten and there was nobody in the writers' building except the stenographers and the switchboard girl. The writers would dribble in anywhere between ten o'clock and noon. I went into the reception room. The switchboard girl turned around and shook my hand and exclaimed over me. She was effusive and she seemed actually glad that I was back. She was good to all the writers and they loved her. She kept out calls from collectors and salesmen. When you wanted a night off, she phoned your wife and said you had been called to a conference and that some old films were going to be shown and it might be all hours. She stalled your girl or lied to your mistress. She listened to the woe and the wrath of grief-stricken creditors and jilted women. Every insurance salesman was a natural blood enemy. Once she bodily threw a tie girl out of the building. She was lovely. She was a sweetheart. We bought her flowers. We kept her supplied with the daily trade journals and the afternoon papers. On Christmas we gave her presents.

"I thought you were taking your lay-off," she said.

"I decided not to."

"It's good to have you back!"

"Thanks."

"Have you heard about your script?"

"No, who'd they give it to?"

"No one," she said. She was elated. "Your producer just wants a few changes and a polish job. He said he'd wait for you. Isn't that wonderful?"

"It's unbelievable!"

"You'll get a solo writing credit!"

"That's swell."

"Credit on a good picture is worth more than money out here."

"I know," I said. "How's the gang?"

She told me about some of them, and then she said: "But Mr. Craig's been very upset."

"Lanny? Why?"

"His wife is in Reno."

"No! How come?"

"You'll have to ask him."

She would tell you the news; not the secrets.

"Well, that's too bad," I said.

"Yes, he's been very upset."

She called my producer's office and his secretary said that he would see me at eleven-thirty.

Lanny Craig came in about twenty minutes later. He didn't stop to say good morning and I just saw his hulking figure as he limped past the switchboard. I lit a cigarette and sat very quietly, thinking; then I got up and walked down to his office. I went in without knocking. His back was turned and when he heard me, he slammed shut a drawer very quickly, and looked around. His face was ashen. His eyes were bloodshot and there were heavy black bags under them. He had aged twenty years. There was nothing friendly about him but when he saw me he opened the drawer again and resumed what he had been doing. He had a bottle of cheap brandy and now he reached for a glass. He paused for a moment and then took a second glass. It was a tumbler. He poured brandy into both of them, his back still turned. He drank his own and poured some more. At last he walked around the desk and sat down. He looked at me and nodded toward the tumbler. I went over and took it and threw myself onto his divan. I didn't say anything. The man was shaking as though he had palsy. I had always considered him boyish but now he was ugly. He seemed to have layers of skin, all of it fat. His face was broad and his shoulders were broad. His hair seemed whiter. He wore a white leather shirt and a neat blue scarf. It was new and not yet wrinkled.

"Where've you been?" he said.

"Around." I sipped at the brandy.

"Seen the papers?"

"No."

48

"It's been all over the papers," he said. I knew he wasn't even thinking of Vicky and I hated his guts. "The old girl left me," he said.

"That's too bad."

He sat down. He smelled the brandy he had poured for himself. "All she needed was an excuse," he went on. "For two years she's been waiting for an excuse. Of course she had plenty but she could never prove them. She was afraid of divorce as long as she couldn't get anything on me. She was afraid I'd get some of her dough." He drank the brandy and wiped his mouth with the back of his hand.

I didn't say anything. The brandy was rank. I put it on the little table beside his portable radio.

"She's had detectives follow me all over town," he said. "I've seen the reports. But there was nothing in them. Even when I was chiseling there was nothing in the reports that would hold up in court. She was so damned afraid I'd sue. And I would have. For a million dollars I'd sue my mother. For even ten percent."

"What was it she finally got on you?"

"Vicky Lynn," he said.

I sat up.

"I'd signed papers making me one of her managers," he went on. "According to the law I'm not a manager. A manager has a license or a decree or some damn thing. It's very technical how signing this paper could get my wife a clean divorce but it did. Her lawyers proved that to my lawyer. My lawyer said there wasn't anything I could do. He said he wouldn't handle a suit unless I paid him in advance because there wasn't a ghost of a chance of collecting."

"This is silly," I said. "I don't follow at all."

"I didn't, either. But there were clauses in the contract we made with Vicky that could be legally interpreted to parallel with adoption papers. That's all right. But Vicky was twenty-two. Try going into court and telling a judge you adopted a pretty twenty-two year old girl, whether three other guys were with you or not."

"They cooked you," I said.

"You're damn right. They crucified me. They said get a jury of plain and simple men and women, and before

49

the lawyers were through our pact with Vicky would sound like she'd been running a cooperative house of prostitution."

"But we would have testified—"

"Sure. And it'd be the scoop of the year for every tabloid in the country. They'd frame our testimony to sound ridiculous. They can do that. Just hint something scummy about Hollywood and everybody in the world will believe it. It would have busted us all right out of the business."

I took a drink of the brandy after all.

"We agreed to so damn many things," he said. "To pay her rent until she got working. To buy and rent clothes for her. To buy groceries if she needed them. To—*oh, hell!* You notice this studio wouldn't touch her? They got wind of what was up and they were afraid of the whole thing. But the rest of the companies didn't know anything about us. All they knew was that here was a swell kid coming up."

"But wasn't there any way out for you?"

"Just one," he said. He was trying to load his pipe with tobacco but his hand shook so much that he gave it up. "My lawyer gave me that. He said Vicky should declare in front of witnesses that I hadn't kept up my part of the contract. To say that she was going to cut me out of it. *Then* if my wife tried anything I could have said I thought I was buying stock in a promotion scheme. I would have had witnesses to say that Vicky herself had thrown me out of the set-up."

"Why didn't you do that?"

He looked at me. "You haven't talked to the cops?"

"No."

"They asked me the same question. They said I'd begged her to do it and she'd refused and I got sore and hit her just under the ear there."

I felt my heart pounding.

"They said I went to her apartment to get her to do this and that was when it happened. You see, I have no alibi for that hour she was murdered."

He said these things very smoothly, as though he feared nothing, but he was already a physical wreck, and now I sat up and watched him. I was tense.

"What *did* happen?" I said.

He had gotten up and now he walked to the other end of the office. His limp irritated me. He pulled a book out of the bookshelf and then shoved it back.

"What happened was this," he said. "I phoned her at Max Epstein's office and explained the whole thing. I said I would be in a bar on Vine Street during the afternoon with my wife and my lawyer and a couple of witnesses. I asked her if she'd come down and go through this act for me. I'd said it'd be her first dramatic rôle and to do it good."

"What'd she say?"

"She was frightened. She said she was very grateful to me and she'd do anything I asked. She said she'd be at the bar by three-thirty."

"She didn't show up?"

"No. My wife kept wanting to go. I had a hell of a time. I kept watching the clock. I talked and talked. I talked and drank until I was sick. Everybody was unnerved. My lawyer was in on what was supposed to happen and he was sweating. It was the most wretched hour I've ever spent. At four-thirty my wife left. I couldn't keep her there any longer. At a quarter of five the witnesses went, and so did my lawyer."

He was walking up and down the office. He talked into his chest. I said:

"What did you do then?"

"I left the bar. It was five of five. The car was in my wife's name and she had taken it. I took a cab to Vicky's apartment. Harry Williams was on the switchboard and he said she wasn't home. I was upset. My nerves were jumping. I ached everywhere. I said he was a liar and I jerked him out from behind the switchboard and made him take me upstairs. But he was right. She wasn't home. I went back downstairs with him and the switchboard was jammed with calls. I kept trying to say something to him. I wanted to leave a message for Vicky. But he was so busy I got disgusted and walked out."

"So there was no message to prove that you had been there at that time," I said, quickly.

"No."

"Did the cops check up to see whether the switchboard was jammed at the time you said?"

"Yes, but the tenants in the building were half nuts and all anxious to exaggerate their own importance. They said the board was clogged from five right on through. They told different stories. The cops didn't get much out of them."

He sat down on the edge of his desk and out of habit picked up the phone. He gave the girl the number of his bookie and then hung up to wait for the call.

I said: "Did anybody say for sure that he heard Williams' voice on the switchboard after five o'clock?"

"No. His voice is like the one of the guy that relieves him and—But what *is* this? Do you—"

His phone rang and he picked it up. He asked about the horses and the odds. I waited. He placed two bets and hung up.

"The odds might change before the race," I said.

"So what?"

I looked at my finger nails. My hand shook.

"Did the cops get rough?"

"No. Why?"

"Nothing," I said, "only they could have worked it out like this: that you went to Vicky's apartment at the time you said. That Vicky didn't want to see you and said she wasn't home. That you pulled this stunt with Williams and went up anyway. You and Williams with the pass key. That Vicky was there and there was a big scene."

"Listen—"

"That would account for Williams' disappearing," I said. "He would have been a witness and after you hit Vicky the cops could say that you had to get him to hell out of the way. The cops would have said it was a motive. A damn good one, too. But sometimes cops don't think of those things. And, of course, there was no clue that put you in the apartment. It wouldn't have held up in court."

He sat there on the desk staring at me. His eyes were terrible. He was breathing hard. He picked up the brandy bottle and emptied it into his glass.

"Anything else," he said. "Have you thought of anything

52

else you can add to it? Go on. *You* might as well cook me. Everybody else has taken a piece out of my hide. Build up a case, honey."

"There's nothing else," I said, "except—"

"Except *what?*" he yelled.

I got up. "Except that you say it was five or after that you went to her apartment."

"That's right."

Our eyes met. "The autopsy showed that she was killed at approximately five o'clock," I said.

I didn't know what he was going to do. He looked down at the glass in his hand and swished the brandy around. He looked up at the wall.

"I know it," he said, "I've been worried. The trouble is the bartender on Vine Street testified I left his place at five of five. I'd been watching the clock all afternoon, and made him conscious of time. They found the cab driver that took me to Vicky's place. He said about five. But it still isn't strong enough for them to arrest me. They'd never get a conviction."

I didn't see why they wouldn't.

"Anyway," he went on, "there's a detective named Ed Cornell. He's in charge of the case and *he* doesn't suspect me." He lifted the brandy. "To Ed Cornell of the cops. To my dear wife who cut me off without a cent. To pals that'd like to hang me!" He drank down the brandy and threw the glass at the wall. It broke and the wood partition of the wall shook.

I saw my producer. He told me the same thing about the script the girl had told me but without frills. He said he was glad I was back in the saddle. The studio would probably pick up my option, he said. I went down the stairs and out through the front entrance and walked along the sidewalk in the sunshine. I went over across the street and had a drink. I drank to Ed Cornell.

Chapter Eight

For two days there were clouds in the sky, and then one morning there were no clouds, but the sky was solid black, and the air was dark and wet. It was muggy hot and it made you sweat. It stayed this way until about noon and then suddenly the sky split open and lightning licked down through, jagged and white, and shuddering with thunder. The windows shook with the thunder. There was a whiff of breeze. Then the rain started. It came down in thick, solid drops, and then it came harder and harder; it came in furious brass sheets and wrapped up the sound stages and clattered in the studio streets. You could see the far off palms swaying in their agony. But the rain was sweet and cool and it was a relief more than anything else. I took my hands off the typewriter and watched it.

I had lunch brought to my office and then I turned on all the lights, closed the windows and went on working. I stopped about four and checked out for the day. My car was parked in a filling station lot about a block from the studio, and I got soaked on the way. I didn't have any top coat. I put papers on the seat of the car and drove to the hotel. As soon as I got in my room I took off all my clothes and took a hot shower, then put on a pair of shorts, my robe and slippers, and sat down on the bed. I sat there for almost an hour reading magazines and then there was a knock at the door. I got up and opened it.

Jill came in. She closed the door. She was wearing a green rain slicker, and a little béret that was wet through. Her hair was bronze and she looked pretty. Her blue eyes seemed very clear. She was breathing heavily and for a moment she said nothing.

"Forgive me for not announcing myself from downstairs," she said now.

"Forget it. Take off your coat."

She took off the slicker and I hung it up in the bathroom where it dripped on the tile. I heard her talking.

"You never answer when I call from downstairs."

I came back into the room. "I haven't been here very much."

"You've never been here when I called?"

"No," I lied.

"It's all right. It doesn't matter. But you might have phoned me." She was wearing white linen. The skirt was tight across her hips.

"I never thought of phoning," I said. "I guess I should have. Cigarette?"

"No. You might have come over to see me." She was watching me intently. "You've got the key. You know the way."

"I guess I should have." I lit up. I shook out the match and put it in the tray on the dresser.

"Why do you keep saying that? You haven't come because you didn't want to."

"No, it wasn't that."

"I've been very lonely," she said. She paused. "I use the word. Lonely."

"I know what it's been, Jill."

"You might have at least telephoned."

"I know. Look, I'll call and get drinks." The rain was coming down very hard, and you could hear the traffic on Vine Street. Jill leaned back up against the door.

"Never mind drinks. Have you seen Ed Cornell?"

I said I had.

"He doesn't believe Harry Williams is guilty."

"That's what he said."

"He thinks it's you."

"He said that, too."

"*Is* it you?"

I called down and ordered two gin slings. I sat on the bed. I pulled my feet up and smoked my cigarette. She came over and sat down on the edge of the bed. She wasn't timid.

"*Is* it you?" she said again.

"Do you think it is?"

She looked at me. "No." She dropped her eyes. "Oh, Peg, I've been so confused!"

"Of course you have."

"I think of it at night. Sometimes I lie in the dark and think of it. Once I dreamed about you. You were running down a long, long corridor. You—you were screaming. I thought then that you had killed her. But all I wanted to do was help you. I kept remembering the way you'd been. So real and—" She looked up, and there were tears in her eyes. She brushed them away. "You see how silly it is? I had to see you. I'll be all right now."

There was a knock on the door and I said come in. The boy brought in the drinks and put them on the dresser. I paid him and he went out. Jill got up and took one of the glasses. She sipped at it. She didn't look at me any more. I got off the bed and went over behind her and took her by the elbow.

"Hello, kid," I said.

"Hello, Peg." She turned around and looked up at me.

"You're pretty swell," I said.

"But you didn't want to see me."

"I do now. It's just—you'd been so close to Vicky. I didn't want to talk to you. I've been a terrible fool. It's going to be different now."

She looked at me and didn't speak. The rain was thick and solid past the window and the room was damp but hot. "Let's drink on it," I said. We touched our glasses, and both of us drank.

I asked her what she was going to do about the apartment and she said she was going to move downstairs in the same building to a single. A friend of hers was coming back from New York and would probably move in with her.

"Who is she?"

"Her name is Wanda," Jill said. "She was an extra here. But she got sick of it. She was friendly with Hurd Evans, by the way. She hated Hollywood. She said you could starve and die here and she went to New York to become a big actress. Now she's trying to scrape up enough money for bus fare."

I pointed out that it wasn't a very good investment to take an apartment with a girl who was coming home from New York broke. There would be the rent to pay and food to buy.

"Oh, she'll manage to get a few days' extra work every month," Jill said. "And I've a job of sorts—three song spots a week with a local radio station."

I looked down at her. She was very pretty. "Jill—why don't you wise up? This Paul. He's got a million dollars and he's young. He isn't bad, is he?"

"No."

"He wants to marry you?"

"He says that."

"Then why don't you—"

She turned away from me "I'll have to be going now."

"Listen—"

"No, you don't understand, Peg."

"I don't understand *what?*"

"That girls keep waiting for—for dreams to come true. That they keep eating cheap hamburger and slapping cheap faces and waiting. There're always lots of ways out. But they aren't any good. Nothing's any good unless you believe it!"

I turned her around and I held her against me, and kissed her. I kissed her full and hard on the lips.

"Go home, baby," I said.

"Peg—" Her eyes were wet.

"Go home. I didn't mean to do that."

I went in and got her slicker and came out and helped her put it on. She kept watching me.

"I want to hold you and kiss you," I said. "But I'm not going to. I don't love you. It would be very splendid to love you, Jill. But I don't. Go home now, kid. I'll come and see you."

"Will you really?"

"Yes," I said.

"Goodbye, Peg."

"Goodbye."

She closed the door and I walked around the room. The rain was black and heavy, and it came down in torrents.

The room was wet and hot. I sat down on the bed. I was trembling. The smell of Jill was still sweet in the air. I couldn't stop thinking of her.

Chapter Nine

The D. A.'s office called me at the studio the next day, and I went down and hopped in my car and drove into Los Angeles as fast as I could. They had already started when I arrived in the room where they had told me to go. Hurd Evans was sitting down at a little wooden table and the assistant D. A. was standing over him asking questions. Besides me, they had sent for Lanny Craig and Robin Ray. There were two or three detectives in the room and one of them was Ed Cornell. He looked at me without expression and then he turned back to the proceedings. I edged in and watched.

Hurd Evans' eyes were almost glassy. His small face was specked with sweat and he kept wiping it away with a nifty red handkerchief. You could see the guy's slave bracelet big as day. The assistant D. A. was the same one who had talked to me. But he was different now. He was nasty.

"You say this idea occurred to you the day before Miss Lynn's screen test?"

"Yes," Hurd Evans said.

"And on the following day you phoned Johnny Wismer about it?"

"Yes."

I had no idea what they were talking about but I saw Johnny Wismer. He looked gaunt and miserable. They had already worked on him and he was messed up a little. His collar was open. There was a pile of ten and twenty dollar bills on the table. Robin Ray's handsome young face was intent. He was watching Hurd Evans. Lanny Craig looked worn out and disinterested.

There was a solid hour of questions and it was a long time before any of it made sense. The assistant D. A. acted like he was in court. He asked Hurd Evans something, then he turned around and snapped out a question to Johnny Wismer.

What had happened was this: On the day before Vicky's screen test Hurd Evans had gotten the brilliant idea that if we insured her for fifty thousand dollars it would be a swell publicity story. He called Johnny Wismer on the following day and asked his opinion. Johnny had told him that it had been done before, but it was always good. Hurd asked if it was necessary to actually take out a policy in order to get such press, and Johnny told him that he could break certain papers and columns with a story but if he wanted really complete coverage he would have to have the policy to back up the story in case anyone wanted to check on it. Hurd then said we'd want complete coverage. That it was a fine story. She was our investment and we were insuring her. He thought it was very Hollywood and very novel. It was the same as a ship builder insures a ship. He asked Johnny to find out how much such a policy would cost and said that we'd just pay the first premium.

Johnny called Hurd back and told him how much it was. An hour later, Johnny got the money by messenger. He was supposed to take out the policy at once and start the story on the wires. But there was a little larceny in Johnny's blood, and he decided he would try and fake the story anyway. So he had put the money in his safe. He had several of the news stories ready to break the next day when Vicky was killed. He naturally cancelled the stories. But he was bewildered and stunned by the tragedy and when Hurd Evans asked him if he'd already laid out the cash for the policy Johnny replied that he had. It never occurred to him then that under the terms Hurd had ordered him to get, the insurance would now be due and payable. After Vicky was buried and Hurd called him and asked what the company was going to do about paying off, Johnny got scared and told the D. A. He confessed to the larceny and they were making no charge against him. This was a murder case and they had no time for larceny.

The point the assistant D. A. stressed now was that Hurd Evans had gone ahead and told Johnny to get this insurance without consulting any of the other three of us. Hurd claimed it slipped his mind but the attorney quickly brought it to his attention that by his own statement he had conceived the idea for the insurance on one day and hadn't called Johnny about it until the next. But Hurd Evans maintained he'd forgotten to tell us. With Vicky getting a screen test there had been a lot of excitement and he simply hadn't remembered. He said he had intended collecting a share from each of us to pay off the premium. He had spent the cash out of his own pocket, knowing he could collect from us later. The attorney asked him if he had any right to spend our money without our permission, and Hurd replied that he hadn't but that he had felt it would be all right.

The important fact seemed to be that after the murder occurred Hurd Evans imagined the money would be paid off; and that at just this time he needed money very badly. The assistant D. A. had checked with the studio and he brought up the fact that Hurd earned two hundred and fifty dollars a week. That isn't very much and Hurd flushed red. You never discuss salary in a studio. You might get two hundred or two thousand. But you never discuss it. Your agent won't. Under ordinary circumstances, there is no way anyone can find out what you make.

"Can't you live on your pay?"

"I live on it all right, yes."

"Then why did you need money?"

"I have an ex-wife who is pressing me for alimony."

"Is that all?"

"No. There is a girl in New York who has written me for money a number of times."

"What's her name?"

"Wanda Hale," Hurd Evans said.

"Why do you feel you have to give her money?"

"I used to go with her. She knows a couple of people in Hollywood. I was afraid she might make trouble for me at the studio."

"What is your bank account, Mr. Evans?"

"I have none."

"You've been living up to every penny?"

"Yes, you have to. You have to give parties. I had some

money saved but I spent it trying to promote Vicky Lynn."

"Promoting Miss Lynn was quite a strain on you?"

"Yes."

"But you didn't want your colleagues to know that you couldn't afford it as well as they?"

"That's right."

"They didn't know how much you earned and you felt you had your prestige to maintain?"

Hurd Evans nodded.

"So with your account depleted and between your ex-wife and Miss Hale you were—shall we say—desperate for money?"

"I—yes."

"So desperate," the assistant D. A. snapped, "that you killed Vicky Lynn!"

"No. That's not true!"

"What did you do with Harry Williams?"

"I don't know anything about him."

"Where were you on the afternoon of the murder?"

"At four o'clock I left my office and went over to Olam's Bar."

"Is that a customary habit?"

"No. I was upset about money."

"What time did you leave Olam's?"

"I don't know. It might have been four-thirty."

"Where did you go then?"

"I drove home. I live in a little house in the Valley."

"Have you any servants?"

"No."

"You live alone?"

"Yes."

"Then there was no one that saw you at home? You might have been there or not. We have only your word?"

"That's right."

"Are you sure you didn't drive out on the Sunset Strip and pick up Vicky Lynn in front of Max Epstein's office?"

"I'm quite sure."

"What did you do with Harry Williams?"

"I said I didn't know anything about him."

"Is that your money on the table?"

"Yes, that's the money I sent Johnny Wismer to pay the insurance premium."

"You thought for this small investment your share when the insurance was paid would be some twelve thousand odd dollars?"

"It didn't occur to me until after she was killed. In the beginning I thought it would be good publicity. I thought the price of the premium was worth the publicity."

Afterward I walked out with Ed Cornell. It wasn't my idea, but he stuck beside me. We walked down First Avenue and over toward Broadway. He wore the same silly derby and a light trench coat. He kept his hands in his pockets.

"Will they hold him?" I asked.

"On what?"

"He had motive."

"You can't hold a man simply on motive," Ed Cornell said. "Besides, there isn't even that. He had a legitimate excuse to take out the insurance. You can only infer motive and that isn't strong at all. If there wasn't that publicity angle and he had taken out insurance on her, it would be a different thing."

"I suppose."

"It's just that the attorney understands insurance. It's very simple for him. He learned it in law school. Money as a cause for murder. But that isn't the motive for the good murders. You didn't murder Vicky for money."

"Listen, that isn't funny any more."

"I'm not saying it for fun."

"Then why don't you prove it? Hurd Evans and Lanny Craig both had wonderful motives but you won't even look at them! You're letting a murder case go to pot because of a personal prejudice!"

"Jealousy is the best motive," Ed Cornell said. "Jealousy causes sudden anger. You were jealous of Robin Ray. Vicky was half in love with him."

He said it very sweetly, and I was too sore to speak.

"Come up with me to my room," he said.

"I don't want to go to your room."

"Vicky's there."

"You're crazy!"

"She's all around the room. There're four pictures on the dresser mirror and six around the walls. I'd like to have you see them."

"Go to hell," I said.

"I will very soon. In about six months. The doctor said six months at the outside. That's if I take it easy."

I looked over at him. "What do you mean?"

"Six months," he said. "That's all I got. The cops don't know. But even if you told them and got me out of the force, I'd get the evidence against you before then."

"Are you *that* sick?"

"I'm walking into my grave," he said. There was a wan smile on his white face. "I'll be very happy in a coffin." He looked up. "There's something else in my room I'd like you to see. It's an effigy."

"An effigy?"

"Of you in the gas chamber," he said.

Chapter Ten

Now, in November, the darkness came at five, and the heat was gone, and the air tasted of cider; but the roses still bloomed and the leaves were green. It was like summer in autumn. It was pleasant and invigorating. There was a sweet, crisp wind, and the nights were deep and blue. It was a lovely Hollywood then. It was like a beautiful studio set full of the sound of music and laughter; it was gaudy with color and action. All up and down the Boulevard the shops were very bright and gay; and you saw the tremendous searchlights moving back and forth through the sky. A preview of a new picture; a new open air market; or a drug store that had just put in a soda fountain. They all hired arc lights.

Fall, and the town was magic! The film trade papers kept you posted about where your friends drank cocktails, and whose wife had better watch her step, and whose option was picked up, or who had checked off the lot. The winding, glorious Sunset Strip sparkled with clubs, the best bands playing The Cloister. Everyone was there after a première. Everyone was someone because just anyone didn't get in.

The nights were getting longer, and the air crisper, and the lights brighter; on sound stages all over town cameras were whirring; dialogue and gunfire and comedy echoed from empty projection rooms; drama and beauty and youth were rushed into tin cans. Typewriters clicked endless reams of publicity. Song writers stood around pianos in their shirt sleeves and somebody played. All right, for the score over the titles, try this theme, swipe a little from Cole Porter. Give me something as good as *All the Way* or *My Foolish Heart*, not half as good, as *good!* Try it this way, no no! That sounds like something out of Peter Gunn; what I want is sweet music. No more original stories. Just books and plays. TV's got all the original stories. TV can have all the original stories. But they can't afford *Exodus;* they can't afford *South Pacific;* they can't buy a *Look Homeward, Angel.* That's our edge. That's our big edge. Big properties for the big screen. The Screen Writer's Guild is having a meeting. Strike vote against independents that won't pay residuals on old movies. What do those writers want these days? Blood? They were paid the first time around and paid good. The independents will make movies without them. Yeah, but how? I'll tell you how. With Method Actors. Those jerks make up their own dialogue. The story, too? Foreign grosses are off. No more B pictures. More B pictures for drive-ins. Monsters and teen-age sex properties. *I Was Raped at Hollywood High.* It'll gross a million. Gross a million and you can make it for spit. What do you mean no more B pictures? No more musicals. Except big musicals. They've got those old Astaire-Rogers pictures on TV now. Why don't we invent a new Astaire-Rogers team? Why doesn't Fox make up its mind whether it's going to make features or turn itself into a TV factory? And what's Metro up to any more? Does anybody know? And what's with Paramount these days? It's a kookie upside down town. But one good thing: everybody's working.

Glamour, personality, emotion, going into tin cans. Dale Robertson on a horse. June Allyson has turned to the TV tube. Entertainment. Grosses. Liz Taylor in a sarong would gross millions. Susan Hayward in a gas chamber broke all box office records. Grosses. Marilyn Monroe. Grosses. Sinatra and Brigitte Bardot. Grosses. Who hates Hedda Hopper? Who loves Hedda Hopper? What's Sidney Skolsky up to these days? So go to Schwab's and find out. This'll break Louella's column. You get a screen credit. You get a big fine wide screen credit. Aren't you lucky? People don't want money. They want big, fine, wide screen credits. Grosses. Grosses. Grosses.

"Hello, Robin. Robin Ray. It's good to see you. Here, move over. Will you have a drink with me, Robin? I'm having champagne. The champagne's so good here."

"I'll have champagne, too."

"You're looking good, Robin. You look bigger and healthier. You've got glamour, kid."

"I've got the jitters."

"What's the matter?"

"Let's face it, old man. My rôles are getting worse. My option's running short."

"Oh, don't worry, you'll get a break. It's always like that."

"I heard you telling a star that. I heard you tell her that she was better looking than Suzy Parker and a better actress than someone else. And the next night I saw you having dinner with the someone else. You writers tell actors the same thing."

"No, Robin. I mean it with you."

"You were saying she was better-looking than Suzy Parker, and it was a rotten lie. She's heavier than Suzy Parker. I don't suppose you remember. But it was my party. There were a lot of people there and you probably forgot it was my party. That's all right because practically everybody else forgot it. Everybody except the people who sent me the bill. I was hoping they'd forget. But they didn't."

"You're bitter, Robin."

"I'm bitter and blue. I've got the Hollywood jitters."

"Here, drink. Cheer up."

"All right, I'll drink. I'll drink to you. I'll drink to the dope that put a new windshield in my car and didn't make it shatter-proof glass so that I damn near killed myself. I'll drink to him."

"Did you break your windshield?"

"That was about a month ago. It just shattered. But I've broken it again since. I stopped too fast, and it broke. It was a sweetheart of a windshield. The next drink's on me. Scotch. Scotch, bartender. Two Scotches. Haig & Haig."

"Do you ever think of Vicky?"

"I think of her all the time."

"Did you love Vicky, Robin?"

"I loved her; yes, Christ help me, I loved her. I said I didn't. Everywhere we went I said I didn't love her. But I did. I loved her. She was sweet. She was fine, wasn't she? Wasn't she fine?"

"She was wonderful."

"I remember the way we went everywhere, and the way the columns linked our names. Juvenile and ingénue. She was swell. And she could be here now. She could be here this Fall. It would be her first year in the inner circle. She'd be dazzled. She'd be blinded. She'd laugh and it'd be like music in a Jackie Gleason album."

"Here're the Scotches. I don't know if I should drink Scotch with champagne."

"Why, of course, Friend. Of course you should. That's the drink of the Hollywood Virgin. Remember? I came up in tails and brought Scotch and champagne and we drank to Vicky?"

"I remember standing her up on the table, and she said—"

"No, don't remember."

"What's the matter?"

"I would rather not remember. I would rather not talk about it. I would rather drink."

"I'll order two more Scotches."

"All right. Two more Scotches. I haven't finished this one yet. Have I told you about my next studio assignment?"

"No."

"I must tell you. It has zest and delicacy. It is a meaty little characterization of a gangster who attempts to make a racket of the fine, clean game of hockey. I am a fine actor. I am a rare young Brando, and this is a choice tidbit suitable to my outstanding ability. It is a stunning vehicle in which my talents are sure to become legend in the mouths of babes from coast to coast. It will be my greatest of all portrayals and I look forward to it as my debut into the sacred realm of class B films. B is for bastard."

"The Scotches are here, Robin."

"Jill, what are you doing here on the lot? And in make-up, baby! God, you're beautiful in make-up!"

"I'm a dress extra."

"That's fine."

"It's not fine. It's $29.04 a day. Wanda's in town—back from New York. She helped me get this job. I had to get myself registered at Central Casting, of course."

"It's getting dark. It gets dark early as hell, doesn't it? Did you ever notice? Here, stand under the light. . . . Christ, you're gorgeous! I like the way that Civil War dress comes down off your shoulders. Look! A milky white canyon . . ."

"Stop it, fresh! I thought you were going to come and see me?"

"I've been busy."

"I noticed that by the trade papers. Who's your press agent, Peg? You get around, don't you? One star and another."

"Jill, for heaven's sake—I—I've been *going* to come up, but—"

"But you've been going around in the champagne waltz, isn't that it? Wyatt Earp rides again . . . and then again . . . and again!"

"Honey, I'll come up tomorrow. No, tonight. What are you doing tonight?"

"Don't do me any favors, Peg! Or is this charity clinic night?"

"But I'd really like—"

"You're much too kind, darling. Really! If you came to see me some nasty little columnist would write 'what star did a burn when what scenarist let her cool her heels in the bar at

Dave Chasen's last night?' You're far too generous with us extras, dear. Have you no class consciousness?"

"Jill, for Christ's sake— Look, how about tomorrow? Tomorrow at about, say—"

"No. I'm going to be busy."

"*Jill*—hey, turn around here! Kid, you're smearing your make-up!"

"It's all right. I—always cry a little when I see old friends. Anyway, I'm through with the make-up. All I've got to do is collect my $29.04 and—"

"Honey, this is so silly! You have that million dollar guy— Paul, isn't that his name? Why, you could have any damn thing you wanted if you played it right with him, if you—"

"Yes, aren't I a fool, though! Thanks for pointing it out. . . . Goodbye, Peg. I should slap your face. But I won't. They're waiting for me in the wardrobe department. I'll see you sometime. Goodbye. . . ."

"Don't worry, Lanny. They'll pick up your option."

"They'll like hell pick it up!"

"Why don't you quit drinking that brandy? It makes your breath stink. If you're soggy with that slop all the time they won't want to pick up your option."

"Listen, pal. Your option hasn't a God damn thing to do with brandy. It's strictly a matter of dialogue. Write hot dialogue and you can lay drunk under your desk for weeks and they'll still hoist your option, see? It's all in—"

"What does your agent say?"

"Nothing. He doesn't answer his phone. But he's a fine fellow. He always trusted me. Only last Christmas I met him at a party. He'd come with his wife. You understand what an awful thing it was, don't you? When he saw me he paled. The man was shaken. He took me off in a corner. 'Listen, Lanny,' he said, 'please, for God's sake, don't tell anybody you saw me out with my wife—my mistress would leave me cold!' So you see how it is. We've always been Like That. I admire him. He's a sport! Brandy?"

"No."

"Hockey is also a sport. Have you ever given pause to meditate on what a fine, clean game it is? No? Nor did the racketeers who muscled in, greedy for the dirt which is money. Not for one minute did they realize the *spirit* of the game! Sir, they were at last coping with something bigger than tommy guns. In the end Jack Armstrong triumphed. A victory for clean living! Shoot if you must this young blond head—but wave the flag for Hudson High, he said!"

"God!"

"Screen play by papa."

"So I gathered. But hell, Lanny—do some TV."

"I've got news for you, buddy-boy. I *have* to be stoned to admit something like this: I've been trying TV on the side. And you know what I found out? This'll shake you. It's tougher than writing movies. Some of those half hour shows even want you to have talent. What gall! Imagine! Anyway—I've spun out seven different half hour scripts and I can't even get *Lassie* to buy one of them!"

"What about your credits?"

"I've got seventeen. I call them the drone of the B's. They won't help. Only your name on decent pictures, on solid grosses, do you good."

"Then write books."

"Do what?"

"Write a book."

"But that's *work!*"

"Oh."

"It'd take me weeks, maybe months. I used to write English mysteries. I'd never been to England but I was young and ambitious. My stuff had something then . . . listen, you bastard, why don't you shuddup?"

"I haven't said a word."

"Just *shuddup!* What'd you come around here for? Did you want to see the Inner Man? Well, I'll show you to him. He stinks. I always knew what he was like but I never had to face him before. Funny, isn't it? It's a little like dying. Funny!"

"Well, Lanny, what—"

"You want to know what I'm going to do? I'll tell you. I'm going back to New York. Snow and slush, freezing winters, a crappy apartment—a walk-up on Charles Street. I'll write for fact detective magazines. A penny, two pennies a word.

When and *if* you peddle. That's the way I began—before I wrote my first book. Now I'll complete the circle. Round trip through paradise! I'll have a portable radio, see, an old typewriter, and a dose of Greenwich Village clap. I'll be fine!—*Brandy?*"

"No."

"I thought I'd ask."

"Hello, Ed Cornell. What goes with you?"

"It goes very well with me, mister. Everything is just dandy."

"You frighten me, Cornell."

"I don't mean to. If you see me around, across the street when you're in a house, or looking in the window when you're at a bar, or walking behind you in the rain, just don't pay any attention. I don't want to scare you."

"Oh, thank you very much."

"It's quite all right, mister. But I think it's only fair that I should warn you that it won't be long now."

"What won't be long?"

"The completion of my case. I'll very soon have enough concrete proof to send you to the gas chamber."

"Goodnight, Cornell. It's been very nice."

"Goodnight, mister."

It is November, and the days are short, and this is Hollywood. The bell is ringing. They're shooting on stage thirteen. The red sign wags back and forth. Don't try to go in while it's wagging. Extras are walking in a group on the studio street. The executive commissary is packed. Over there is Sophia Loren. Isn't she lovely? Across the street the song writers are going crazy. They've got a new tune. It'll be on the hit parade. Outside the cutting room you can hear the sound of film being run through. Snatches of dialogue scream out at you. Laughter and the sound of a car starting up. A producer and a director are playing ping pong in the studio gym. You hear the balls ticking back and forth. The red sign on stage ten is wagging now. They're shooting. A truck goes by with carpenters in it. The air is crisp and it tastes fine. Here comes a cute kid surrounded by half a dozen flunkeys. It's hard to believe she's a big star. But she is. She's box office. Her pictures gross.

"Hello, guy."

"Hello, darling."

"See you tonight?"

"Sure."

Chapter Eleven

For a while I escaped. I remember now that for a long time I wasn't myself. I was a guy caught up in a glorious vortex. I was mad and gay and that isn't me at all. I was in the middle of a silver cyclone and the days and the nights whirled by with a shrill musical screaming. I was a guy in evening dress. Champagne's bright child. I was carried along in a clique of crazy people and I didn't have to think. I dined here. I slept there. Table conversation, with a sparkle. Splendid bedrooms, and dialogue in the dark. Breakfasts at noon. It was fun. I thought it would never end.

But I began thinking of Jill. I tried to fight it but I couldn't. I didn't want to see her. I didn't want to hear her name. But in the middle of a party I would think of her. I would think of the night she sat and listened while I told her how we were going to build up Vicky. I would think of her in my hotel room, wearing that damp linen dress that was tight on her hips. I would think of her in grease paint and a Civil War costume. When I drove in my car and saw the palms and the stars I remembered her. When I kissed girls that didn't mean anything to me at all I remembered Jill. I don't know why. Because I hated her. I was scared, thinking of her. Maybe *she* killed Vicky! Maybe it was Jill! I was crazy. It was insanity to think like that. And yet I did not know why I was afraid of her!

It was as though I could feel her naked arms around my neck pulling me down . . . down and out of my golden cloud. The glamour dissolved from silver into steam. The world was sordid and ugly and I felt Jill dragging me down. I walked along the street; and I kept feeling that she was trying to pull me into the curb. It was a psychosis that stifled my breathing. She became an obsession. I was frightened. I didn't know what was the matter with me. I hadn't seen her again nor heard from her. But she was with me night and day. Once I was lucid and I thought it was like a voodoo hex. I thought that she was deliberately thinking of me and doing this to me.

I didn't like this and I stayed away from her. There is a coward's philosophy that time heals all wounds. Cover up your ugly deeds with days; pile the days on and on until the deed is buried deep. But Jill kept rising out of the grave of these days. It became worse. I would remember verbatim things she had said. I drank, but whiskey no longer lifted me. Twice I ran into Ed Cornell. I ran smack into him on the street. I do not remember what he said either time. I didn't think about him after he was gone. I thought only of Jill. I couldn't eat. I forced sandwiches and malted milks into my belly but I couldn't eat. There were nights in my room when I walked up and down and tried to make myself decide to go and see her. But my fear grew with the obsession. I had a horror that I would some day run into her on the street.

Then I could stand it no longer. I thought I was losing my mind. There was no reason why I shouldn't see her. I drove over to the apartment. For a long time I sat outside in the car trembling. Then I got out. I felt numb. I walked in and asked the boy at the switchboard for Jill. He announced me and I went up.

The apartment was a one-room single on the second floor. The windows faced the building next door and it was dark. It was not nearly as nice as the other apartment. I had been in so many fine places. This was sordid. The divan was a wine red. The bed folded into the wall. There was a table, and flowers in a vase. The flowers were wilted. The room was hot and I smelled cooking. Jill had opened the door. She was wearing a red silk dress and an apron over it. She had a pancake turner in her hand. She didn't say hello and I didn't speak. Now she stood in the middle of the room and looked at me. The electric light was dim. Then there was a voice from the kitchen.

"Bring him in, Jill."

Jill didn't say anything. I walked over to the little kitchen and looked in. A tall, straight-haired brunette was sitting at the table. She was thin and her face was hard. I don't think she was pretty but she was in thick motion picture make-up and she looked pretty. She glanced up at me.

"Hello."

"Hello," I said.

Jill went past me and over to the stove. She took out some hamburger and put it on plates. She gave this girl one of the plates. The girl looked at Jill and then at me and laughed. It was a short laugh.

"What's the matter with you two?"

"Nothing," I said.

The girl gazed at me. "I'm Wanda Hale."

"Jill's spoken of you."

"I've got a job tonight," she said. "I won't be here long."

Jill was doing something at the sink. She was trembling.

"I've got a job at U-I," Wanda Hale said. "Some night scenes."

Jill didn't look at me. She sat down and pretended to eat. She got up again and fetched the coffee and poured it in two cups. She sipped the coffee black.

"You get time and a half at night," Wanda Hale said. "I like to work at night."

"I'm not averse to night work myself."

"Sometimes there's a party afterwards," Wanda said.

"Yum. Yum."

Wanda ate her hamburger. "Sit down," she said.

But I kept standing. I leaned against the door jamb.

"Something ought to be done about extras," Wanda said. "They've made it a racket. One guy said we were just like migrant field workers. But if they give us a job they come around and take away half of the pay envelope. There are men that make a living that way."

"I've heard that. Nice boys!"

"Sure," Wanda said, "straight from the Young Men's Earnest Endeavor. They worked their way up from pimps. But if you don't cut back you don't work!"

"It's either a cut or nothing."

"It's either a cut or a God-damned empty stomach!" Wanda said. "Starvation. But one day there'll be a payoff. You can kick a dog only so long, you know!"

"I'd rather kick a cat. It's safer."

"The extras," said Wanda, "they get the crap. But it can't last forever!"

"Certainly not. God will protect the working girl."

"You're funny, aren't you, mister? Well, it's *our* lives! It ain't funny to us!"

"I'm sorry."

"*Sorry!* A helluva lot you care!"

"What do you want me to do—wave a tambourine?"

"You write, don't you?"

"Only plays," I said.

"And you don't care anyway; the only ones that really care haven't the talent to tell it on paper. The only ones that care are the ones that eat dog food and live out their miserable lives here, hoping to hell they get a break. And if they get a break they don't care any more. But some of us will always be extras and this is our lives."

"You're going to be late, Wanda," Jill said.

"Some sweet day a John Steinbeck will come and tell about it," said Wanda. "He'll tell about it because it'll make him money. But he'll tell. The way guys are beaten up because they don't want to give their dough to racketeers. How girls have to sleep with fat slobs to get work. How girls get pregnant and climb the hills and jump off the Hollywoodland sign."

Wanda squeezed out from behind the table now and got to her feet. "I've got to go," she said. "It's too bad you don't care. Maybe you could tell it. It would take a very long book. But you have to care. Otherwise it'll just sound cheap and dirty."

She left the kitchen and went to a closet and got her coat. I looked at Jill but Jill was sipping at the coffee and wouldn't look up. Wanda Hale was in the middle of the room now. Her face glowed with the grease paint. She had a little round hat stuck back on her head. She held a purse in her hand.

"Do you ever see Hurd Evans?"

"Sometimes," I said.

"I don't," she said. "He won't see me. I wired him for money when I was in New York. He didn't send it, but now he won't see me."

"I'll tell him I saw you."

"Never mind." She went to the door. "It's too bad you don't care. A lot of silly things have been written about Hollywood. But nobody's ever written the real book yet."

"It isn't my line," I said.

"No. It would take an older guy. A guy with ulcers in his stomach and acid in his heart. Too bad Horace McCoy died. He could have done it. He wrote a sweet book when he wrote *They Shoot Horses, Don't They?* Somebody ought to re-print it."

"Yeah. It was a fine book."

"I'm glad I met you. I've got to go now."

"Goodbye," I said.

"It's really too bad you don't care," she said. Then she went out and closed the door.

"Nice girl," I said.

Jill didn't say anything. She had finished her coffee and was looking into the empty cup. She was trembling. The hamburger was untouched on her plate. I sat down. I slipped a cigarette out of its pack and began fooling around with it. Jill was very pretty. There was color in her face. Her breasts were hard against the red dress as she breathed.

"You shouldn't have come," she said. She said it so low I scarcely heard.

"Why not?"

"You shouldn't have come."

"You wanted me to," I said.

"No."

"You were thinking of me."

"That's something else," she said. "I didn't want you here."

"Why not?"

"I don't know," she said.

"A long time ago Vicky said you were in love with me."

"It wasn't true. It isn't love."

"What is it?"

75

"I don't know," she said.

"You're trembling."

"I wish you'd go."

She scared me. "You've been talking to Ed Cornell again," I said.

"Yes."

"You shouldn't listen to him, Jill. He's an hysterical fool."

"Yes, he is."

"Lanny, Hurd and Robin each had excellent motives to kill Vicky."

"I know."

"But he won't consider them."

She looked up. "It isn't Ed Cornell. That isn't what's wrong with me."

"Then what is it?"

"I don't know. I keep thinking of you. I don't know why I should. It started even before Vicky was killed. It started the first time I ever looked at you. You came into the room, and I was there and you stopped and we stared at one another. It was as though—we'd met before. It gave me a chill."

"I remember," I said. "But I didn't know you'd felt that way."

"Now I remember you all the time. And I hate you. But I have an insane impulse that makes me want to protect you. I don't know why. It's just there. It's like you're afraid in the dark and I'm telling you it's all right." She paused. "Worse than that—and this is the hideous part—it's as though these things all took place somewhere before."

I felt icy cold.

"At first I thought it was love," she said. "I'd never loved anyone outside my family. But you aroused me. I kept wanting to see you. I kept wondering what you were doing. But in the past few weeks it seems to be repulsion and hatred. It's like hatred, yet—" She leaned forward. "Are you ever afraid in the dark, Peg?"

"Jill, stop it!"

"It isn't pleasant," she said. "It's turned my life into hell. Perhaps it'll be better now that I've said it all. I don't know why I should want to protect you. You don't need it."

"No."

"Do you think we can forget?"

"I think so. I think so now. You had to say some ugly things. Ugly things get in your soul and make you wretched. It's because you've been under a terrible strain. Vicky's death, and everything. You've imagined these things."

"That must be it."

"If you felt anything toward me before—before Vicky was killed—that was just natural. It happens with a certain boy and a certain girl sometimes."

"Yes—I guess so."

"Because nothing's going to happen to me," I said.

"No."

"Ed Cornell's just hysterical."

"Sure."

"Let's have a drink, Jill."

"All right; we've got some wine. It isn't very good."

"That'll be all right. I'll bring some good wine when I come again. Listen, that Wanda Hale's a nice kid."

"She's had a tough time," Jill said.

"Sure, I can see that. Shall we go in the other room and drink the wine? This kitchen's stuffy."

We sat on the divan. The wine was cheap and we didn't drink much of it. But it was something to do with our hands. The room was depressing. The ceiling was low and the building next door seemed very close to the windows. Jill turned on the radio and there was a dance band. The bulbs in the electric globes were twenty-five watt and they were very dim. I was afraid of Jill and I talked much about nothing. Then she got up to get a book to show me. She walked across the room. She had a lovely body. I got up and she handed me the book and I put it down. She looked at me, frightened. But we just stood there. I was shaking visibly. I reached up with one hand and turned off the lights. For a moment it seemed very dark. I could hear her breathing. But I couldn't move. My heart was beating so fast that I had to lean against the wall. I wanted to turn the lights back on but I didn't have the strength to lift my hand. I thought I was going to collapse. I felt hollow all through.

Now she came to me. She didn't touch me but she stood very close. I knew I was a fool, but I couldn't move. I felt cold sweat on my face. She put her hands on my shoulders and put her face very close to mine. Now I could see her. I imagined I could. I drew her hands down. My throat swelled up with a scream. I choked it off. But hysteria kept coming up through my chest.

"Jill—you look like Vicky!"

"Do I, darling?"

"You look exactly like Vicky in the dark!"

"You must be wrong."

"No, you do. Jill—*I'm afraid!*"

"Are you afraid, darling?"

"Jill—"

She put her lips against mine. It was all right then. It was just for a moment that I was scared and now it was all over. But my heart was still pounding. Her lips were wet and her tongue was hot. I picked her up in my arms and carried her across the room. In the dark she was clinging to me, her fingers gouging into my skin.

Chapter Twelve

It was a fine California winter, the days bright and warm, and the nights crisp with wind and crystal clear. I bought a season ticket for the Coliseum and Jill and I went every Saturday. We'd sit in the bleachers, a blanket over our legs, cheering for the Trojans until we were hoarse; after the game we'd hie ourselves to Nikabob's and sit side by side at the bar, devouring popcorn and drinking Bacardis. Jill'd float a fluffy popped corn on her pink Bacardi. "White sails in the sunset." Then we'd talk about the game. "Wasn't that last touchdown a pretty thing, though!" At night we danced at the Biltmore Bowl or the Zebra Room; and on Wednesday afternoons I got away from the studio and we'd drive to Santa Anita. But sometimes, even as a winner thundered across the finish line, we'd never know it.

"You're getting lipstick!"

"To hell with it!"

"Darling, we *are* at a race track! Your hand is—"

"—under your coat."

"Aren't you lecherous, though!"

"Insatiably so!"

"So am I."

"But not as much as me."

"Oh, yes, I am. More!"

"I say you aren't."

"But, darling, I am!"

"Then what are we doing here?"

"I don't know."

"Where would you like to go, Miss Lynn?"

"Any place. Not a tourist camp, though."

"How about a Pomona hotel?"

"No—I don't like hotels. I'd feel cheap."

"Then I'm afraid we'll have to wait til it's dark—and find a plot of grass in the Civic Square."

"Why, Mr. Pegasus—the very thing!"

"Certainly!"

On Sunday we rigged ourselves in official ski clothes I'd bought, and we went over to "a place in the Valley" and skied down a trail of pine needles. The pine was as slick as ice; but there was no snow anywhere about. Once we rode horseback on the Santa Monica bridle path, nodding at Rock Hudson and Tuesday Weld; but afterwards we ached so that we had to stand up at a chicken emporium in the Valley, eating off a chin-high ledge, our riding habits greasy and our hands sticky. We laughed like fools about it. We kissed right there in the restaurant. It didn't matter who saw us.

"They'll get used to this," I said. "My option's been taken up at the studio."

"Has it, Peg? *Really?*"

I nodded. "Just today. I was keeping it for a surprise. It means a jump in pay and six more months here in Glamour Junction."

"How wonderful!"

"Do we celebrate?"

"Of course!" she said.

"Champagne?"

"What else?"

One week-end we hiked up Mt. Lowe, both of us puffing, and blowing steam. Jill's breasts were bunched against a thick sweater, and her face was rosy and her eyes very bright; when it was night we sat in a little rented cabin on top of the mountain, watching the softly falling snow.

A few days later we splashed in the shiny blue surf at Malibu, and lay in the white sand, Jill wearing a tight yellow bathing suit, just one piece. I remember coming into the beach cottage once just as she was changing. She grabbed up a towel and covered herself with it.

"Please!"

"You're lovely, Jill."

"Peg, go 'way. I'll be right out." She was shivering.

"But, mommy, I'm romantic!"

"Darling, I'll be rheumatic if you don't go!"

"Okay; I'm bribed. But how 'bout a kiss?"

One evening we decided to drive down to Laguna for dinner, but the car raced through the night, making scarcely a sound, and we went on to San Diego. It was a navy town, and it was gay and bright and festive. The streets were thick with sailors and girls. *Welcome Navy* signs appeared everywhere. Night clubs blazed with color; inside, pretty painted girls in star-spangled tights, danced in choruses, and sailors whistled and stomped. The Plaza was all lit up, trolleys clanging by, and every few minutes a stripped-down Ford, crammed with sailors and girls, skidded around a corner. Fords, motor-cycles and girls. The fleet was in.

Jill and I ate dinner and drove to the harbor. Warships lay at anchor, side by side. Destroyers, four abreast; long sleek submarines; cruisers and tenders. Their yardarms blinked; searchlights combed the sky. A night squadron of Navy Boeings roared overhead. Now and then we heard the echo of a bugle; and water taxis and motor launches kept coming in at the dock, disgorging uniformed men. The lights of Coronado flickered on the opposite shore.

"California's beautiful, isn't it? It's pretty . . . and has sunshine, and some very nice people in it."

"—Such as Jill Lynn."

"You're sweet! Only—"

"What?"

"I was thinking of Vicky."

"Oh."

"Do you ever remember, Peg?"

"You should ask: do you ever forget? Because I don't."

"She'll always be between us, won't she? No matter what fun we ever have. We both loved her, and she'll be there . . ."

"Jill?"

"Yes?"

"I—want you to know something." I was turned toward her, my elbow on the steering wheel. "Vicky was tops. She was all honey and silver. She was laughter at midnight. Only she wasn't the first girl I ever had—maybe the nicest 'til you, but not the first . . . see? And you *are* the first, because it's all different. . . . I love you more than going to bed. I—Christ, this is a lousy speech, isn't it? I'm supposed to be so eloquent. But I don't know how else to tell you!"

She was looking down. "It's—nice of you to say that, darling. Even if you don't mean it."

"But I do!"

She was crying suddenly. "Do you know—I believe it!"

"Drive, darling," she said a bit later. "Drive along the shore."

"Okay, and you sing."

"Sure. I'll sing—I'll sing like Jerry Colonna!"

I drove down the long ribbon of road, the headlights glowing through the night, and Jill sang. The sky was silver with dawn when we arrived back in Hollywood. The streets were still and the rows of tall palms stood like lonely totems. I pulled up to the apartment and walked to the door with her.

"Can I come up?"

"Darling, Wanda's there."

"If that's the sad state of affairs—get some sleep. USC's

playing in the Coliseum today. I'll be over at one and we'll rush through breakfast."

The dawn was bright and new and I felt swell. I walked back to the car, whistling.

Ed Cornell was sitting in the front seat.

Chapter Thirteen

"Not Ed Cornell," I said. "Not the celebrated Temple Street nemesis!"

But he didn't even look up. He wore a thin, shabby top coat, and he sat there shivering, his hands jammed in the pockets.

"Isn't it rather early in the morning for ghouls, Mr. Cornell?"

No soap. His white face was gaunt and haggard. He was the most morose bastard I've ever seen. I walked around and climbed into the car. I stuck a cigarette in my mouth and lit it. My fine mood was going to hell fast. I tried once more, feebly.

"Good old Cornell," I said, "crêpe(s) of wrath. Look, Operator 13, don't you think you've followed That Man long enough?"

"I'll always follow you," he said. "This is your murder story, pal. This is the one that don't end happy."

"This is the one that's true."

"Yeah. I've been waiting for you since midnight. I kept thinking you'd show up—then when you didn't it got me sore. I decided to wait you out."

"For Christ's sake!"

"I know. Always living in the garbage cans of somebody else's life. I scavenge old souls." He raised his head. "I was over there—across the street. You didn't even see me when you drove up."

"I wasn't looking for you. What do you want?"

"The usual things. I've run into quite a lot of damaging evidence just following you around. I don't look for it. All I do is keep track of you and it comes to me."

"The Cornell method."

"Yes—without portfolio." He coughed again, and talked through it: "You—you can drive me—to my hotel—if you will."

"Will you stop coughing!"

"I can't help it. A touch of T.B., you know; and I think I've caught pneumonia waiting for you. The buses haven't begun running yet. I can't afford taxi fare. It's five miles."

"You've got guts, I'll say that."

"I can't help it. I've spent too much of my own money following you already. They won't give me an expense account. It's all my own time, and my own dough."

"I'm crying."

"But I imagine they'll reimburse me when I bring in the material for your trial. They usually do in these cases. I nick a guy on my own time and send him up to the chamber—and then I get back pay." He had begun snuffling. The sound made me itch. "You'll drive me, won't you?" He blew his nose and looked at what was in the handkerchief. "If you're stopped for speeding I could probably fix the ticket." He wadded the handkerchief and put it back in his pocket.

I started the car and drove off. I hated his high-pitched voice. It was a sort of nasal tenor, all one tone. The car reached Western and I made a wide turn, the tires squealing.

"I hope it isn't pneumonia," said Ed Cornell. "That would be a crappy thing, all right, wouldn't it? I shouldn't have waited for you so long. There was nothing to gain standing there."

"Naturally not."

"It'd be a hell of a thing to get pneumonia—and be in bed in a hot room with a lot of bottles. I've got you just about where I want you and this is no time to stop. I could arrest you today, for that matter, but you'd get some hot shot lawyer and you might wriggle out with life instead of the death penalty."

"Have you any idea what the hell you're talking about?"

He nodded. "A kind of running knowledge. I've been in the business a long time. I've already got plenty of evidence

83

on you. Just hung around the places you went, and it fell in my lap. I could take you to court tomorrow. But I still need a strong motive. I'm fairly sure I know what it is but I can't prove it yet."

The wet tires sirened on the black asphalt. I said: "*What* evidence have you got?"

"Enough, mister. Don't worry about that. And I'll have the motive in a week or two. It's going to take some doing—getting the witnesses lined up—but I'll do it."

"You're crazy!"

"Sure. You say that. That's why I can tell you these things. I don't scare you enough to make you commit suicide. And if you ran away they'd only get you again. A little man—a clerk or a butcher—he can hide for a while, but a guy so dumb he can only make dough writing words on paper—he ain't got a chance."

"No?"

"No. You make money and you forget how to live. You'd be screwed trying to live like a human being. You'd tip your hand—and wonder how in the hell you happened to do it."

"I see."

"They all think I'm nuts," Ed Cornell went on. "And I never get tired seeing the surprise when we come up with Exhibits A to Z. Some of them scream. A few faint. A lot of them just get pale and light a cigarette with a trembling hand—like in a mystery. Maybe they say some crappy thing like: 'The jigs up, gentlemen.' They always say something they'd never say at any other time. For one little minute they've got a spotlight, and—scared as they are—they turn ham actor. But up in the death cell they look kind of pitiful. A human being never believes his own death is justified—no matter what he's done. He's spent his life from childhood doing wrong things and getting Just One More Chance—everybody is like that. God will forgive you. But the law won't: and the victim finds it subconsciously unbelievable. That's why some of them hang on and don't crack. Up to the last minute they're convinced they'll get another chance."

"Why do you tell me these things?"

"To persuade you that I'm not crazy. I'm just—well, inevitable. Like death. You'll never escape me."

"Listen—" I sucked for breath. "Listen—God damn it, I'm not guilty of anything! If—if you persecute me it'll be wrong. Your mind is warped, and I don't know what you intend to do—but whatever it is, it'll be wrong!"

"Thank you, mister."

"For what? What are you talking about?"

"That's the first time you've flattered my ego with fear. I've made progress. You've never admitted before you thought I was capable of anything."

"Progress! Your silly attempts to wear me down. You can't hypnotize me! Do you think you can? You're whacky!"

"Perhaps—but inevitable."

"—you!"

"Vicky and I—in our room—we think of you at night."

"Why, you dirty, degenerate bastard!"

There was a bus on Seventh Avenue and I raced a block ahead and stopped. I reached over and opened the door.

"You can catch the bus," I said.

"Very well, mister. Thank you for the ride. I hope you aren't angry. I'm only following my conscience to the—"

I jerked the door out of his hand and slammed it shut.

"That's very queer," the assistant D. A. said. "Cornell has said nothing at all to me about you. Some of the boys suspected you in the beginning, and since then there's been a flurry of interest in Hurd Evans—because of the money angle. But this office had concentrated on Harry Williams.

"Obviously, Williams has skipped the state. A crime of passion is generally committed by a man of his low mental caliber. We pin our suspicions upon him entirely. If he were innocent—why should he run away?" The attorney paused. "He won't get far," he went on smugly. "No, sir. We've got dodgers throughout the country." He picked up a fact detective magazine. "Got an article about him with a picture—in here. Take a look at it."

I opened the book and my hands shook. There was a lewd morgue picture of Vicky. I couldn't bring my eyes up;

they were hot with steam. My heart hammered at my chest.

"Wrote the article myself," the lawyer went on. "Pick up a few dollars every month that way."

I threw the magazine across the room and got to my feet. "You dirty son of a bitch!"

He stared up at me—stunned.

"You dirty swine!" I was half choking.

"Why—it's just—we always do that—and—"

"Is there nothing sacred to you, you two-bit bastard!"

"I don't know what you're talking about!"

It was useless; he was *so* stupid! He was assigned to Vicky's murder, but he was only one of maybe half a dozen assistant district attorneys. He was a hundred-dollar-a-week heel with a mind in which only the very obvious was understandable.

"You're a ghoul," I said. "You pimp corpses."

It was all Greek to him. I walked to the window. The magazine lay at my feet, the page open. There was a fly buzzing on the windowpane. The lawyer went on talking, very nervously:

"Ed Cornell has no right to molest a citizen. He has no orders from the police to go near you. Of course, he's doing it on his own time."

"What the hell do I care whose time he's doing it on?"

"I quite understand how you feel. I—I appreciate your emotions."

"You do like hell," I said. I squashed out the fly with my thumb. It was a big blue fly with white guts and I had to wipe my hand on a handkerchief.

"Ah—you seem upset."

I turned around. "Do I?"

"Yes." He was playing with a pencil. "And isn't it strange Ed Cornell should bother you? He has taken a similar interest in cases of this sort in the past. Working quietly on his own—not a word to us, mind you. But he's never failed to turn in a brilliant case record. Once he's started on a man's trail he's never failed to bring him in with evidence enough for a conviction." He paused. "He's a queer chap, all right. One track mind—with a cyanide pellet at the end of the track."

86

"Look, sweetheart, are you by any chance implying that—"

"Of course not! I'm terribly sorry!" He rattled the pencil. "I was reflecting on Mr. Cornell. I wasn't necessarily considering you. Naturally, he is wrong this time. He's only human and certainly he can be wrong."

"There's always a first time," I said. I said it before he could say it, and to keep him from saying it, because I could feel it coming.

"Exactly. You word things so well!"

(Oh, God!)

"I guess that comes from being a writer."

(You want to hit a man as stupid as that.)

"Of course, I write a little myself."

"Let's not go into what *you* write," I said.

"Ah—no. Let's not. Won't you sit down?"

"I'd rather stand."

"It's possible"—he went on slowly now, thinking very hard—"that Ed Cornell is railroading you."

"What do you mean?"

"I've seen it happen," he said.

He was a fine, intelligent attorney. I sat down.

"How? Tell me how?"

"A cop gets a suspicion in which he thoroughly believes —but there's no evidence. So he goes around and builds evidence. He finds little things that look incriminating. What he can't find, he invents from whole cloth. He forgives himself for this because he sincerely thinks his victim is guilty and it's the old story of planting phony money on a man you know to be a counterfeiter. You have to have proof for the courtroom."

"I see," I said. He wasn't so bad; he was all right in his own shop, I thought. Every man is all right in his own shop.

"It is possible to build a case out of nothing," he continued. "It takes time and intelligence—both of which Cornell has. Time and brains. To demonstrate what I mean: how often have you heard of an innocent man serving time for say—murder—only to be pardoned when the actual killer signs a confession? The killer, dying, or indicted for another crime, reveals the truth. The innocent man is freed. But did you ever stop to consider the insurmountable evidence there must have been against the *innocent* party to send him up in the first place?"

"Go on," I said.

"That's all. The police believed the innocent victim guilty —and because they couldn't get a conviction otherwise, they built up a case. I don't say that it happens very often, but it's quite possible."

"Does it take the police to do it?"

"No, a lawyer could do it. Or any man could if he took the time to engineer details that would stand up under the microscope of logic."

"And that's what Ed Cornell is doing to me?" I shuddered. "I can almost feel him throwing the dirt on my coffin. Every day another spadeful."

"I don't say that's what he's doing. Naturally such a thought is small comfort to you. Because we will surely prosecute to the hilt if he brings in a case, I may as well tell you that."

"You mean to say—"

"We'll check the facts, naturally. This office isn't against you. But this office badly needs a conviction for the Vicky Lynn murder, and so much time has gone by that I'm afraid—"

"You're afraid you won't be very particular?"

"Well—"

"You'd just as soon convict me, and close the books."

"I didn't say that."

"Convict me and write another article," I said. "What about Harry Williams?"

"I imagine we'd have to assume he was dead if—"

"You make me sick," I said.

"Well, Ed Cornell *can* be wrong. But the fact is—"

"He's never been wrong yet!"

"I was just going to say that. How did you know?"

Chapter Fourteen

On Hollywood Boulevard all of the street signs were changed, and now they read "Santa Claus Lane." On every lamppost as far as the eye could reach there were gay, colored Christmas trees, very fat and laden with silver, blinking with lights, rich and bright and happy. In a tinsel archway that made a bridge over the street were golden bells and tiny figures of Santa Claus, and bulbs, red and green and yellow; and reindeer, the gayest, dizziest reindeer you've ever seen, and red holly berries, and green wreaths, and white, artificial snow. It was as though Santa Claus Lane was a magic tunnel, festooned with beauty, the splendid, endless line of Christmas trees its radiant, painted walls.

At night people came from everywhere to see Santa Claus Lane; they packed the sidewalks, they jammed the streets. They crowded into the bright shops, for the shops all stayed open. Pretty shops full of lingerie and champagne and boxes of candied fruits and shiny red tricycles and electric trains and new TV sets and spacemen suits and toy sailboats. Shops all decorated with Christmas, dolled up like pretty girls, doors open wide, every clerk busy, wrapping packages in scarlet and blue and silver paper. And there were little fruit markets with arc lights swinging back and forth at the curb in front of them. And there were theaters, the Chinese, across from the Roosevelt Hotel, and the Egyptian, marquees sparkling, and book stores with bright, eye-catching window display, and newsstands gaudy with Christmas issues.

"Darling, this is a nice café. But I'm not hungry at all. I'm just kind of tired. It's—nice sitting here where you can rest—and sort of watch the boulevard."

"Yes—God, look at those mobs!"

"Uh-huh. And everyone has bundles under his arms. Presents . . ."

"From Oscar with greetings—"

"From Aunt Minnie with love. . . ."

"Makes you feel warm, doesn't it, Peg? Christmas always makes me like this. I'm all full of songs like a little hurdy-gurdy."

"Sell me a carol."

"Sure, Peg, what kind?"

"—Channing."

"Oh, that's terrible!"

"I know. Damn it. Jill, maybe we'd better eat."

"I'm not hungry. You eat."

"I'm not hungry."

"Then let's just sit here. The champagne's good—and my feet are so tired!"

"Shall I order a bottle of champagne?"

"No. This is fine. Look out there, Peg. That hunchback midget selling his papers."

"He's a landmark."

"Oh, darling, this is a lovely night!"

"Jill—"

"Yes?"

"Let's get married!"

"When?"

"Tonight. We'll fly to—"

"No—in January. The old year's been sad. I'd rather start new."

"It's a date, Miss Lynn. New Year's Eve in Las Vegas!"

"Oh, that's thrilling!"

"Think so?"

"*Think so!*"

"Merry Christmas then—from me to you, with love."

"What is it? . . . Peg! Oh, darling! It's such a *beautiful* ring! When did you get it? Such a gorgeous diamond . . . !"

"Hey, Jill, you're crying . . ."

"Shut up, you idiot! Don't you know Christmas isn't for eight days yet? Eight more shopping days— Look, the ring fits!"

"Must be some mistake. I'll send it back."

"Over my dead body!"

The sky was gray and heavy, and the lot was quiet, the little streets dark and empty, and yet it was a fraud, for the sound stages were alive; you could see the wagging signal and the light flashing red. The office buildings were lighted up and bursting with sound. *Five More Shopping Days*. The hysteria has begun. Holiday time. We're crazy. We're all a little crazy. Hollywood Christmas. *Drink with me!* Doors were wide open. Radios were going: *Sweet Lalanai won at Santa Anita to pay $3.20*. There was a running crap game in 411. Secretaries were everywhere. *Merry Christmas*. Or is it Christmas yet? *Five More Shopping Days*.

"Where's Lanny Craig?"

"Over on stage ten."

"Is it an open set?"

"Sure, it's a B hive. They're shooting a space thing. Nobody over there knows what outer space is but they're shooting a space picture."

Outside of the door of stage ten the red signal was wagging, and I waited, and then I went in, opening the padded, soundproof double doors, bolting them after me with the big dog winches. Almost the moment I was inside the bell sounded again and they had resumed shooting. I stood very still, afraid to breathe lest the microphone should pick it up. The set stood at a right angle and I could see about half of it. The heavy lights played down on an office desk, behind which, in make-up, stood Oscar Markoff, a fine character actor whom the studio had greatly over-worked.

Markoff stood behind the desk, his face flushed with grease paint. He was apparently concluding a telephone conversation, and as he set down the phone the door of the small set opened. Robin Ray, wearing the outfit of an astronaut, came striding in.

Oscar Markoff

I thought you were out in space by now.

Robin Ray

The rocket ship has been sabotaged. Strange things have been going on.

91

I heard Hurd Evans' irritable, haranguing voice.

"Cut. God damn it, cut!"

The main arc lights snapped off and I moved forward. I could see the whole set now. The camera—a huge, square box, cameramen sitting on small seats on either side of it—was on tracks. The moment Robin Ray had entered the door of the set it had registered him in a *Close Shot* and then immediately trucked back with him as he crossed the room. But Robin had crossed the set at a slight angle and as he had reached the desk the camera had pivoted on its axis and wiped to a *Close Two Shot*, side angle, favoring Robin Ray. It was in this position as the dialogue started, and its mechanism had clicked off, leaving it here.

Hurd Evans sat up on a high stool near the camera. He was wearing gray slacks and an open shirt. His brown hair was stringy and his face was covered with sweat. They'd evidently been over this one scene a number of times. The props men and the electricians, planted around the set, and perched in roosts on top of it where they directed dozens of overhead lights, looked worn and disgusted. I didn't see Lanny Craig.

"What was wrong?"

"What was wrong? God damn it, Robin. You can't even remember one line at a time, can you?"

Oscar Markoff, quiet and resigned, sat down.

"Shall we get you an off-stage blackboard? When great artists blow up we try to assist them, you know."

"You don't have to get nasty," Robin Ray said. He looked very young and handsome in the heavy, tan make-up. He looked like a champion of outer space.

"The line is," said Hurd Evans, "'strange and *mysterious* things are going on.'"

"Well, it stinks."

Lanny Craig stumbled onto the set. His huge bulk swayed unsteadily. He needed a shave. His eyes were dilated. He stared at Robin Ray.

"Maybe you'd like to rewrite it?"

Robin looked at him contemptuously. "Why don't you go lie down?"

"It's lyrical. Saroyan never equaled it."

"Saroyan stinks," said Robin.

"Sure. He stinks a Pulitzer Prize worth. He hasn't any form. He peddles vitality. I peddle fish. If you've got oomph, it doesn't make any difference how you write. But if he had vitality and ever learned to plot he'd be one of the great ones. Shakespeare wasn't too good to use a plot. I'm going to get a plot. I'm going to get a plot in Forest Lawn."

"Saroyan smells," said Robin.

Lanny wiped the back of his hand across his mouth. "What the hell do you know about it? What does a two-bit actor know about anything but his face? For my dough I'll take Rod Serling. Serling is a sweetheart on paper."

"For Christ's sake, shut up!" Robin said.

"We're only trying to make a picture," said Hurd Evans.

"You run off at the mouth," Robin told Lanny. "You're washed up here. Why don't you get out of a studio where you're not wanted?"

Lanny Craig looked as though he were going to fall down. "This is my last picture and—" He stopped. "You son of a bitch," he said.

I went into the set and led him away. I tried to get him out of the sound stage but he wouldn't go. He sat down on a box and belched. He began to cry, silently, unreasonably. Hurd Evans was talking and the lights came back on very bright. I heard the buzzer "Roll 'em," and the clacking noise. The sound man, seated at his machine, wearing ear phones, said: "Scene twenty-three, take seven." Then Oscar Markoff was talking on the phone again. Robin Ray made another entrance. The dialogue commenced.

Robin Ray
—strange and mysterious things are happening.

"Cut—damn it! Cut!"

Everyone was upset and it went on like this. There was no glamour. It was tedious, uninspiring labor. The manufactured art going into tin cans. And yet it was not of these things I thought now. I was thinking of Lanny Craig, sitting there, tears on his flushed and mottled face, hiccoughing softly. *He imagined Vicky had broken up his million-dollar marriage. He had been in the apartment the very hour she was murdered.* I saw Hurd Evans, distracted and nervous, sitting on the high stool. *He had needed money. He is always in jams with women. He had insured Vicky for fifty thousand dollars.* I shuddered and looked over at Robin Ray. The handsome lad: but clumsy with women notwithstanding. *He'd loved Vicky, hadn't he? He had loved her desperately.*

There was an aching all through me, and I laughed. It was all so incredible. Harry Williams, that was it. The switchboard boy. A crime of passion—and he had skipped. Subject matter for fact detective magazines. These things happened. This other, this mean suspicion, was born of the fetid thing fear. Holiday hysteria. *But what if Harry Williams, too, was dead? What if he lay rotting in some shallow grave?* I was cold and sick.

"Back to New York," Lanny Craig mumbled, "snow and steam heat."

"*Scene twenty-three, take nine.*"

"*Mysterious things are going on. There are far stranger things in outer space than earth has ever dreamed of.*"

"My heart's in the highlands," whispered Lanny. "That's sweet, sweet dialogue!"

"Cut," said Hurd Evans.

What if Harry Williams, too, had been murdered?

I felt a tap against my arm. It was a messenger. "There's a guy on the lot looking for you," he said.

"Who?"

"I don't know. Funny guy, though. He must be drunk. He says he's going to arrest you for murder."

Chapter Fifteen

"He says what?"

"That he's going to arrest you for murder. He must be full of hops."

"Is his name Ed Cornell?"

"He didn't say."

It's Cornell all right. He's completed his case. It must be a

94

pretty thing. And he'll put you in the gas chamber! Don't fret about that. He's been after you for a long time. You can scream until your lungs rot. It won't do any good now.

"What did he look like?"

"Kind of white around the gills. Red hair, I think. He wears a derby."

It hit me all at once. I was so scared I couldn't stand up. I found a box. My hands were shaking. I was hollow. I was so scared that I was sick. My teeth began aching, the way they ached that night. All of my teeth ached and hurt my mouth. I thought it was funny my teeth always ached when I was scared. I didn't have any other coherent thought. I was empty like a sack is empty.

The scene was going on. There was Robin Ray in an astronaut suit. There was Hurd Evans sitting on his stool. Lanny Craig was drunk and sleeping. Cornell couldn't get into the sound stage while the camera was in motion. He'd have to wait out there until the red flag stopped wagging. There was a side door.

I knew there was this side door. But I couldn't move. Now the scene ended. If Cornell had come in with handcuffs I still wouldn't have been able to move. I was trying to get my breath. My hands groped in my pocket for a cigarette. *Where were those damned cigarettes?*

I remembered things: "I have an effigy of you in the gas chamber. . . ." And: "Some of them scream. . . ."

But I'm innocent, I tell you I'm innocent! Does it mean nothing to you that I'm innocent?

"No, it means nothing to me," he'd say, "because I don't believe you."

I had the cigarette now. I mashed it between my fingers before I could get it into my mouth. I threw it down on the floor. I looked at it and rubbed the sole of my shoe over it.

Then I was on my feet. I didn't know how I was able to stand up. I felt as though I had been in a hospital for six weeks, and this was the first time I had walked. There was a ringing in my ears. *Merry Christmas,* people would say. *You're a cooked goose. We're very sorry for you.*

Wasn't it too bad about him, though? This they would say afterward. *He was such a nice chap. Didn't look like a murderer, did he? I was at the trial. They had a beautiful case. A really beautiful case. The prosecution was brilliant. He's in the death house now. They say he's writing letters to everyone he knows. He writes fine letters but they won't do him any good. He's going to die on Wednesday. I see by the papers—*

I was at the side door. My hands shook so that I could scarcely throw back the bolts. Then I had the door open and fresh air was sucking into the sound stage. I got outside. I didn't wait to close the door. I wanted to run. But you can't run on such wobbly legs. *Run where?* Where in the hell would I run?

Why should I run? I'm innocent! He can't do this to me! Who in the hell does he think he is that he can do this to me? I'll go back and laugh in his face. He can't prove a thing. Theories, maybe. What's a goddam theory? I'm not scared. I'll face him. You damn well know I'll face him!

But I wouldn't. I couldn't take the chance. It was my life at stake. You don't gamble with your life when you have odds like these. Let's be realistic. Nobody wants to die.

I was in the studio street. I was watching for Cornell. A strange, stolid calm was settling over me like a block of ice. If I caught sight of him I could bolt. I kept walking. I was conscious of my footsteps. Each step was taking me a little nearer to freedom. Each step was taking me a little farther from death.

The darkness had come. It was black and lovely. The little studio lights were on. I could hear film being ground through in a projection room. It was only five-thirty. Dark winter evening. The secretaries were streaming out of buildings and going toward the main gate.

They'd go home. Go on dates. They'd eat their dinners. They'd complain about headaches. They'd study shorthand, go to movies.

I was on the sidewalk, headed toward the main gate. The secretaries had formed a little queue and were punching out. You could hear the bell on the time clock. The girls were chatting, and going out the gate in pairs, or in threes. Cars were waiting out in front for some of them, clogging the street. Guys in Fords, or old Chevrolets. These were the great writers and actors of tomorrow, these guys, who let their wives support them until the Big Day came. Only for almost all of them the Big Day would never come. They'd never even make their first dime. But it was all right because the married secretary went on for years imagining she had a Rock Hudson or a Mort Sahl in her home, and she could be smug as hell, and life would be worth living. This was the way of Hollywood. Up your sleeve or in your shoe you had a dream.

I suddenly hated them all. I felt detached, and it seemed to me that this picture was sordid. The glamour . . . and the greed for glamour. The petty hatreds, and the broken hearts, and the bums that hung on, the bums that cluttered up the cafés just outside the gate. Once they'd been extras, and while they were on the set, if they could so much as mooch a cigarette from a director, they'd spend the next six weeks off the lot writing notes and sending them in. *"Listen, pal, old pal, I need two bucks. Will you send your old pal out two bucks?"*

I walked right through the main gate. Nobody stopped me. Cornell must have been somewhere on the lot. I crossed the street. There they were, the midgets and the hunchbacks; the Hawaiians and Filipinos, the white females who couldn't even pass as extras, all hoping to run into somebody now at five-thirty, hoping to buttonhole somebody who could promise them a job. Behind me secretaries were getting into cars. Others were walking on up the street. I was *safe!* I was lost in this crowd. The winter darkness was good to me.

But I didn't know what to do. I didn't have any plans. My car was in a parking lot on the corner, but I didn't dare take it. It would be too easy to spot. The special body, the blue upholstery, the shiny spotlight. There was a cab on the corner. I moved toward it. Somebody yelled at me. My heart froze.

But it was another writer.

"Can I take you anywhere?"

"No, thanks."

"What about having a drink?"

"I just had one."

I had to move in between the cars in the parking lot. I had to pretend that I was going to get my car out. I didn't know if this guy was watching. But when I turned around he was gone. I began threading my way out through the parked cars. The attendant spotted me.

"Hi, ya! Want your bus?"

"I'm going back to the studio for something," I said.

He'd have to move the cars in front to get mine out and he was happy that I didn't want it now.

"Okay."

"I'll be back later," I said.

I stood on the corner for a minute. I waited until the parking attendant was busy. Then I slipped into a cab. I gave the driver the name of my hotel and slumped down in the seat. The cab pulled out into the avenue. It was thick with cars. Half of them were studio people who might spot me. I stayed down in the seat. The cab got stuck in the traffic and the driver kept honking the horn.

"You can't get anywhere this time of night," he said.

"No."

"They ought to do something about it."

"Yeah."

My heart was going like a hammer. I was fumbling around for another cigarette. I'd try and get this one between my lips before I broke it to pieces. My fingers were shaking. Now the cab began to move. I heard the purr of tires, and we were weaving in and out between cars.

I got the cigarette lit and the smoke drifted between my teeth. Christ, *how they ache!* Maybe it was because I was chattering. Was I chattering? I'd have to get hold of myself. I'd get nowhere with my nerves like this. They'd nab me in an hour.

Cornell would have the alarm out. If he had his evidence it would all be official now. The cat and mouse game was over.

We were on Vine. I didn't know how long we had been riding. The cab was going fast. *It'd be sweet if we ran into somebody.* I could see that happening, and crime reporters harking back to that old, old cliché about the irony of life. *Fate took a hand tonight as—*

But we hit no one and I was watching signal lights change from red to green, and the people that swarmed the streets, and those big, fat, open air markets. I saw the Christmas tinsel, and the big sign that said *Five More Shopping Days!* Sure, so what the hell! I threw out my cigarette and leaned forward. The cab was pulling up. I fumbled with a dollar bill, and got it into the driver's hand. Then he reached back and opened the door. On the Coast, the cab doors are fixed so you can't open them from inside. They aren't opened until the fare is paid.

It's so lovely here!

I got out and crossed the sidewalk to the hotel. The lobby was crowded. But it suddenly struck me what a fool I was! The cops would expect me to come back here. They'd have someone waiting just in case I eluded Ed Cornell. I glanced around. I wanted to make a break back out the door. I saw a flabby-faced guy leaning against the partition between the elevators; he was twirling a key ring.

Yet I didn't know him. He was a cop but I had never seen him before. No doubt he had a description of me. But those police descriptions are like a jigsaw puzzle. He'd have to put it all together. And right now he wasn't even looking my way.

I needed money. I had less than twenty dollars in my wallet. I moved to a writing desk, sat down, and scribbled a check. When I was finished, the cop between the elevators was still there. I got up and walked across to the grilled window marked *Cashier*.

"I wonder if I could get a little cash?"

A girl wearing horn-rimmed glasses looked at me. I took my credit card out of my wallet and dropped it there beside the check. I was trying to smile. But I was so pale I must have looked sick.

"Oh, yes." She read my name. She reached for the cash drawer, and then she glanced at my name again. When her eyes came up they looked funny under the panes of her glasses.

"Just a minute," she said.

"Sure."

She left her cubicle and moved toward the desk. I turned on my heel and started in the direction of the revolving door. My heart was going so fast I couldn't breathe.

The cops had tipped off the hotel! They would probably

notify the big sap at the elevators. But I wasn't having any. *No thanks, sister!* I pushed through the doors. I arrived out on the sidewalk in a cold sweat. People were moving about me. I started for the corner. Then I made a run for a cab. I got in and slammed the door.

The driver turned around and stared at me.

If I don't give him an address he'll think it's fishy. If I just say "drive" he'll think I'm running from somebody.

I gave him the address of Jill's apartment. I didn't know why. I wasn't even thinking now. I sat back, and tried to pretend I was a human being. The cab angled out of its place by the curb. I watched the sidewalk. I saw the big detective blustering through the crowd toward the corner. Sweat dripped off my face.

The cab crawled into a space in the stopped traffic, waiting for the signal. We were parallel with the corner. We had traveled at the same speed the cop was walking. He stood at the corner now, looking around. He wasn't three feet from me! His hands were on his hips and his coat was thrown back. I could see the .45 in his gun holster. He had been chewing gum and he took the wad out of his mouth and flicked it to the gutter.

He glanced toward the cab just as we started up. We shot across the street, the driver trying to beat the other cars in the traffic line-up, grinding hell out of the gears. I looked through the back window. The cop was crossing the street. He hadn't seen me! There were a lot of Christmas lights and a mob of people.

We careened into a right turn and rolled around the bend, up to Franklin.

For a single moment I had the uncanny feeling that I had lived this scene before. And then it came to me, and I escaped out of time.

I was in my own car, on my way to see Vicky. Vicky and I would go on a date and we'd have a fine evening. We'd argue about where we were going to have dinner, because we could never decide. There must have been a thousand places but we could never pick one romantic enough, and we'd drive and drive until our stomachs ached with terrible emptiness, and then we'd end up in some shabby café on

Vermont. There'd be candlelight, and second-rate people, and champagne cocktails for only one twenty-five. But the steaks would be delicious, cooked just right, and Vicky would laugh, the way she used to laugh.

Vicky, who killed you? Who in the name of God could want to kill you? We were never meant for the tabloids, baby.

The cab stopped in front of the apartment. I had the right change out and dropped it into the driver's hand. He opened the door for me. I crossed the little walk, and into the apartment foyer out of habit. There was a boy on the switchboard, and no one else around.

The switchboard kid plugged in Jill's phone and announced me.

"She says come right up."

"Is there any one else there? Any man, I mean?"

"No," he said. "At least I didn't see anyone."

I could take a chance! I had to see her!

I couldn't go away without that. I went up the stairs three at a time, and then down the hall. I knocked at the door.

Ed Cornell opened it.

Chapter Sixteen

He didn't look any different, just tired. The old derby was shoved back a little, and the white skin of his face seemed dead. He was so frail that his vest hung loose, too big for him. His eyes were dull. There was no light of victory in them, no surprise. It was as though he had expected me to show up.

"Hello," he said.

A big, heavy-shouldered plain clothes man stepped out from around the corner. He moved up, jerked my wrists together. There was a click, and I was wearing handcuffs. I looked down at them. The big detective backed up and leaned against the wall, watching me. He made a sucking sound against his teeth, and stuck a toothpick between his lips. I glanced from him back to Ed Cornell.

"This is it, mister," he said.

"But, *listen*—"

"You're to be held without bail. I've arranged that. The trial will commence almost at once—quietly. The studios want no publicity. You'll be in the death house before—"

"*Listen,* how—did you know—I was coming *here?*"

I felt as though I needed crutches to prop me up. I was too sick for argument.

"I know *everything* you're going to do," Ed Cornell said. He talked in the old way, that dry, nasal voice, the tone of which never changed. "I know you like a book, mister. There's *nothing* about you I don't know. You and Vicky Lynn."

I was whispering. "Honest, Cornell. Honest, I didn't kill her!"

"No—of course not!"

He started coughing. He coughed into a handkerchief. He stuck the handkerchief back in his pocket. He was a sick man. He didn't have any strength at all.

"We may as well get moving," he said.

"Wait a minute."

"For what?"

I swallowed. "I'd just like to see—" I nodded toward the door. "You won't mind?"

Ed Cornell shot the plain clothes man a look. "We'll be out in a minute, Harris. This guy's my baby. I've got to wet nurse him a little."

He stepped back from the door then, and motioned with his head for me to go in.

When I was inside Ed Cornell closed the door and leaned against it. I came into the room with my arms in a *V*, the way my wrists were linked.

Jill sat limply in a big cushioned chair. Her face was deathly white, and her hair looked yellow. She wore a green dress, and green sandals. Her face came up, and her eyes searched mine. We just looked at one another. There was in her look misery and compassion and tenderness. The silence was terrible. On the street below a truck was going by. Ed Cornell began to talk. He was still at the door behind me.

102

"It wasn't her fault . . . the kid sending you up. We told him what to say when you came in."

See, her eyes said, *see, darling?*

"I would have nabbed you on the studio lot," Cornell went on, "but the cops have a deal with film executives. They don't want any arrests on the lot, or even near it. They have trouble enough with the press. You know how it is." He paused. "But I suppose you thought you were smart. I guess maybe you thought you were getting away with something . . ."

Jill was motionless, immobile, watching me. *God, she's beautiful!*

"So I sent one of the messengers to say I was looking for you. If you stopped to reason . . . no cop about to make an arrest would announce it like that. I simply wanted to get you off the lot. You were a cinch to either come here or go to the hotel. We had you both places. I *know* you, mister. You wouldn't have skipped town without—"

"*Shuddup!*" I said.

Jill's eyes were watching mine. I spoke to her.

"You—you don't believe him, do you?"

"No."

"You believe me? You believe I'm innocent, don't you?"

"Yes."

"And I swear to you it's true!"

"But he says—you haven't got a chance."

"No." I turned on Cornell. It didn't seem to matter so much now. "This guy's so smart!"

I waited, and Ed Cornell watched me. I didn't take my eyes off him. But I was talking to Jill.

"Haven't you heard about him? He gets perfectly marvelous cases into court. Foolproof. He knows all about chains of evidence and temperamental D. A.'s." I sucked in my breath. The handcuffs cut into my wrists, and I could feel my pulse throbbing against the iron. "What have you got, Cornell? Tell me what you've got. Not theory, understand. But *material* proof! You haven't got any of that, have you? You've just got a swell story. Fine, phony logic for the jury."

"Do you think I'm trying to railroad you?"

103

"That's exactly what I think."

"Well, I'm not. I've never done that. I've always had such proof there could be no doubt. Neither time nor investigation has ever unproved a single thing I ever established!"

Jill got up. "Aren't you wonderful though, Mr. Cornell?"

She crossed to the windows. There was a breeze rattling cocoa fronds and you could hear the traffic on Franklin Avenue.

I glanced back at Cornell. The color in his cheeks had died. The derby was still pushed back. There were little beads of sweat on his forehead.

"Do you think I'm lying, mister? Do you think I can't back up what I say?"

I couldn't answer.

"Do you think I've worked all this time," he said, "to have the thing fall through? No. You were intensely jealous of Vicky Lynn. Do you admit it? It doesn't matter. It's already established. I have witnesses who'll testify to it. *Friends* of yours."

The room was a vacuum. I was putting pressure against the handcuffs. For no reason, except that I wanted to feel pain other than the ache that was in my teeth.

"You're emotional . . . you were jealous almost to the point of insanity."

"That's not true."

"But it is. There's a line in one of your Broadway plays to the effect that a man would kill for the woman he loves."

"Oh, my God!"

"It'll make a fine point for the prosecution," Ed Cornell said. "You know how juries are. But there's *material* stuff to back it up. I'm telling you all this so you'll know what you face. So this girl will know what a liar you are."

"What material stuff?"

"Of letters you've written, things you've said. I'll have a raft of witnesses. Secretaries and hotel desk clerks . . . a shoe shine man, a movie star. Never knew you talked so much, did you? But with a little prodding, people remembered the things you said."

"You put the words in their mouth!"

"Perhaps . . . to help them remember."

"You're a fake . . . and you admit it!"

"No," Ed Cornell said, "it was simply a job of building up an air-tight case. There's the real proof, too. On the day Vicky Lynn was getting her screen test you wrote her a note. You said that she was your day and night obsession. You said there wasn't anything without her. You said *if she loved Robin Ray, you'd want to kill her!*"

Jill turned from the window.

I was watching Cornell. I remembered the note. I had written it at the studio, in my office, on that awful rainy day Vicky was being tested. *It was just the day before she was murdered!* But I'd never sent it. I'd balled it up and jammed it in the pocket of my suit.

I'd worn the suit only because it was raining that day. It was an old suit, and it had hung in the closet ever since. Cornell must have searched my hotel room and found it.

"That fixes the motive," he said.

"But *anybody* might have written a note like that," I said. "It was just—"

"I have the rest, too," he went on. "I've figured out what your route must have been on the day of the murder. I've made a little diagram . . . which I'll present to the jury. You didn't show up at the studio that day, remember? They pay you almost a hundred and twenty-five dollars a day for your services . . . figuring a five and a half day week. But you didn't show up . . ."

"I was upset."

"Certainly! The jury will love that! What man isn't upset on the day he commits murder! And you have no alibi for the way you spent your time. Nobody saw you in the places you claimed you went. Particularly in the afternoon!"

"No, but—"

"It was the apartment upstairs. You arrived early in the afternoon. You had a key. Vicky had given it to you! Have you missed the key lately? I found it in your hotel room one day—and pieced this whole thing together after that! That little key was the solution, mister!"

Jill crossed the room, restlessly.

"You let yourself in with that key. The apartment was

105

empty and you decided to wait for Vicky. This was between three and five in the afternoon. Lanny Craig arrived at five o'clock with the switchboard kid in tow. At that very moment you were hidden in one of the closets."

"That's fantastic!"

"Is it? I have a shoe that belonged to Vicky. It had been in the closet. Somebody had stood on it and it's all crushed. Moreoever there was a cigarette stub mashed out in a corner of the closet. It was found there directly after the murder. I still have it." He looked at me coldly. "You wanted material evidence. I've got a barrel of it. All little bits like this. But linked together—"

Jill suddenly walked to a closet door, turned the key in the lock, and put the key in her pocket. Her unexplained movement upset Cornell and he watched her curiously. She walked past him and out into the kitchen. I heard running water. Then I saw her drinking from a glass.

Good Lord! Doesn't she even care?

"Well, we'll get this over," Cornell said. "I'll construct the picture briefly. There's lots more to it. But this'll do:

"You were in the apartment when Vicky came in. There was a bitter scene over Robin Ray. In a fit of jealous rage you killed her." He paused. "But the very fact that you were in the apartment *waiting,* that you wrote her the note, that you had in your possession the lethal weapon with which to kill—"

"The—*lethal weapon?*"

Ed Cornell nodded. "All of these things add up to the one word: *premeditated.* That promotes the murder to the first class degree, and fries you in oil. Nothing you could say or do would get you off on a second degree charge. You see how it is?"

The iron bands were burning against my wrists. In the kitchen Jill was taking in the garbage pail. At least it sounded that way. You could hear her banging around.

"After the murder you left the apartment," Cornell went on. "But you met Harry Williams in the hall. He had gotten rid of Lanny Craig only a few minutes before and he was still excited. He had come up to tell Vicky about the incident. You were on the spot. Williams would testify he'd

106

seen you leaving the scene of crime. You had to get him out of the way."

"It doesn't matter," I said. I was thinking of Jill.

"It does to me," said Cornell. "It matters a hell of a lot . . . Williams, naturally, was unaware that you had killed Vicky. You bribed or scared him into going downstairs with you. You got him into your car. You drove off to a quiet spot and killed him . . . the same way you killed Vicky. After that you buried him. Probably in the Hollywood Hills, or Laurel Canyon. Once we get you to headquarters, mister, you're going to tell us *exactly* where!"

Jill had come back into the room. There was a row of books on the writing desk and she fussed about, straightening them up. I remember one of the books was *Fast Company.*

"You figured," Cornell said, "that it'd look as though Williams had done the murder and lammed. That was a sweet touch. The night we arrested you, you told the story of how Williams had been in love with Vicky. It'll sound swell when we tell the jury how you tried to sell us that one!"

"But *how* did I kill these people? What's this lethal weapon that you—"

"You don't remember?"

"No!

"Brass knucks," Ed Cornell said. "They were the first thing I came across when I searched through your stuff. Remember Vicky was hit just behind the ear, with a weapon the size of a fist, but much harder—"

I felt as though I were going to collapse. If I'd held out any hope that I could puncture his story, it was gone. I had bought the brass knucks in a hock shop on Main Street, meaning to send them East as a Christmas present for a friend.

I could see the whole set-up. It would look as though I had bought the things for the express purpose of murder. Nobody would ever believe that they were antiques . . . and that I had a friend who collected and cherished such things. Even if I could prove it, it'd sound like an alibi . . . a weak one. Cornell's case was complete. I was finished. *I was through!*

He watched me for a minute, his face very white.

"You're not going to scream, or ask for a cigarette?"

I dropped my head, and looked down at the handcuffs.

"Aren't you going to say the jig's up, and—"

"Let's get going," I said. "You don't have to make it any worse. You've got everything you want. Let's just get the hell out of here . . ."

He shrugged, and turned to open the door.

I saw Jill move across the room. My eyes came up. I saw the thing in her hand. I tried to shout but it was too late. She'd knocked Cornell's derby off, and came down with a terrific blow at the base of his skull. She was using a flat, metal bookend.

In one horrible, petrified moment—something in the way she struck the blow, just the flick of her arm—swept the scene from my eyes and put another one there. The apartment upstairs—Vicky! I shook my head groggily. The scene went away.

Instead Ed Cornell was there. His knees buckled. His eyes flickered, and he looked at me. Jill was backing up. I saw blood run in a little stream down around Cornell's neck. 'Til the very last moment he kept watching me, almost as though he were shaking his head, repeating again and again *You'll never get away.* Then he hit the carpet with a thud. Jill was bending over him, her eyes burning.

"He'll be all right. A doctor told me once how to hit a person."

A doctor told her once. *God!*

I moved toward her, my wrists shackled. Then the words began to tumble out:

"Jill, *listen*—you can't—can't do this! It makes you an accomplice! Besides, there's another detective in the hall. He—"

She looked up. Her face was white and strained. But there was no hysteria. *She had planned this!* While Ed Cornell talked she had worked it all out. She had known exactly what she was going to do.

"He'll be all right," she said. "You've got to get out!"

Cornell was moving; his arm jerked nervously.

I looked around.

"The kitchen," she said. "The cubicle where we put the trash at night to be picked up. There's a door that opens on the hall. You can squeeze through."

"But this other cop—"

"I'll take care of him," she said. "I'll meet you on the steps."

"Jill—" I was wretched. "I *can't* let you do this! I can't—"

"*Hurry!*" she said.

I looked at her. I took both of her hands and kissed them. The iron cuffs were tight against my wrists. Now I turned.

I beat it for the kitchen.

Chapter Seventeen

She had pulled in the garbage pail, and the cupboard door was open. It was just large enough to crawl through.

But I waited.

In the other room Jill had opened the door. She was calling the detective in from the hall. I heard her say:

"He's in there, officer! In the bedroom!"

Bedroom?

The apartment had none, of course. But the detective didn't know it. He was already throwing his shoulders against the closet door. I got down on my hands and knees and began wriggling through the cubby hole. The handcuffs made it awkward. My hands thumped in a wood-chopping motion.

I landed out in the hall and struggled to my feet.

The apartment door stood open and I could see the detective crashing against the closet door. Jill slipped into the hall. The cop was so busy he didn't notice.

Jill joined me, and I followed her down the stairs to a side exit. She opened it, then we were out on the street. Cars were swishing by on Franklin. Jill was catching her breath, looking both ways for a taxi.

These damn shackles!

"Come on," she said.

We started in the direction of Western Avenue. It was four blocks, and the sidewalks were dark. There was a steady stream of traffic on Franklin. Jill and I were half running. Somebody was out walking his dog and we slowed down our gait as we passed him. The guy turned around and stared after us.

"Do you suppose he saw—"

We stopped. Jill gazed down at the handcuffs. Her breasts rose and fell as she breathed. I was wearing slacks and a tan sports coat. Jill studied the situation, then she jerked the coat back off my shoulders. She had me duck down, and taking the back of my coat she swung it up over my head. It was off now, except the bottom of the sleeves, and it hung in front of me. It was turned inside out, but she folded it neatly.

With a little imagination it would seem as though—because it was a hot night, which it wasn't—I was carrying my coat. The way you sit with your coat in your lap at a baseball game.

The handcuffs were entirely hidden!

I just looked at her. There wasn't time to talk. We were both out of breath. We started off again.

A block from Western a siren screamed in our ears. We stood back up against a dark store front. A police car, the siren going, red headlights shining, raced past, headed for the apartment.

The detective must have discovered the ruse. I could imagine the look on his face when he turned around and saw that Jill was gone! He had undoubtedly grabbed for a phone. It was a radio patrol car that had swept past. They'd have three or four of them combing the streets in this neighborhood looking for us. They probably didn't expect that I'd get far wearing handcuffs. They'd send men to cover hardware stores right off the bat.

We reached Western.

"Walk slowly," Jill said.

We crossed the sidewalk and she opened the door of a taxicab. I got in and she climbed in beside me.

"Sixth and Vermont," she said.

The driver stepped on the starter. I thought the motor

would never turn over! Then we were moving up Western Avenue. Another siren scream burst upon us. The taxi hauled over to the curb, and let the police car pass. Now we were rolling again.

"Jill—"

"Yes, darling?"

"Will you put a cigarette in my mouth? They're in my side pocket."

She lit the cigarette for me and put it between my lips. The cab had turned on Sunset and was going in the direction of Vermont. I could lift the locked wrists up to my face and handle the cigarette all right.

"Why'd you do it?"

"You mustn't talk," she said.

"He can't hear. Not with that glass partition closed."

"There's no use taking chances," she said. She was very calm.

"Why'd you do it? I've got to know!"

She looked at me. "Don't you know already? Can't you even guess?"

"Sure, but—"

"Then keep still, darling!"

"I can't! You shouldn't have done it, Jill! Do you know what the cops will do to you for this? Do you know what it *means?*"

"Of course I do!"

"It's such a mess," I said. "What are we going to do?"

"Why, darling, you can grow a beard and we'll work in the mills the rest of our lives! I—*Oh, Lord!*"

"What's the matter?"

"My ring!" she said. "Our engagement ring . . . I was washing out some stockings when Ed Cornell came and I'd taken it off. It's back there on the bathroom shelf!"

"Shall we go back?"

"Darling, it's serious! We could have pawned it. How much money have you?"

"Just a few bucks," I said.

"I've got fifteen dollars."

"Oh, hell, then, we're practically set for life."

"Don't worry, Peg! We'll be all right."

"Sure, we'll be swell!—But we won't. We're used to one kind of life—and there's no escape for us. You know that, don't you?"

"No, I don't know it, darling. And I'm not one bit afraid. I'll never be afraid as long as I'm with you."

"You're so sweet . . . ! Where was Wanda tonight?"

"Working," Jill said.

"A good thing."

"No. She would have helped us. She's that kind of person."

"One vote for Nikita Khrushchev."

"You can't blame her for being bitter."

"No—I guess she's had a rotten time of it. We'll send her a Christmas card from Tahiti."

"How nice!"

"Then when she gets hungry she can eat it."

"Peg, you're horrible!"

"Why not? What the hell am I doing in a jam like this? And why did I have to get you in it? After all that bastard's evidence how can even *you* trust me?"

"Because I would anyway. But also, I know that Vicky intended to give up Robin Ray. She told me."

Suddenly that was a scene too: *Vicky telling Jill she was going to give up Robin Ray.* I had a hell of a headache. I couldn't think any more.

"Did you tell Cornell she said that?"

"Yes. He didn't believe it. He said I was shielding you."

"He didn't want to believe it." I sucked for breath. "Now what's going to happen? You shouldn't have gotten into this!"

"But I wanted to!"

I nodded. "One day I'll thank you for it. I can't tonight. I haven't any emotion left. It's all washed out. I just feel kind of sick at my stomach. Like there isn't anything left in me."

"I know."

"No, you don't. You can't know. You go all your life believing in justice. That right will triumph. Then it's all pulled out from under you. When I was a kid I used to believe in Santa Claus. I think I felt something like this when they told me the truth."

112

"Oh, Peg!"

"Throw the cigarette out for me, will you? Thanks . . . It *is* good having you here. I don't know what I would have done. Gone to court and yelled my God-damn lungs out, I guess. Let them beat the hell out of me in that third degree they put me through before. I've still got scars on my hand where they burned me with cigarettes. I don't know where we'll go. But we'll get married. See, Jill, we'll—"

"No, we won't."

I looked up.

"They'd find us right away if we tried to get married," she said. "Don't worry about that." She looked at me. "Are you cold without your coat, darling?"

I was shivering.

"I wish I could get these bracelets off."

"We'll buy a file," she said.

"No. We'll get a room somewhere and you can pick the lock with a hairpin. I'll show you how."

"Aren't you smart, though?"

"Sure. I'm smart. Raffles, that's me!"

We got out of the taxi at Sixth and Vermont, and as soon as it drove off we got another one. In this cab we raced into downtown Los Angeles. Jill figured we should get out of town before the cops covered the bus terminals and railroad stations. We paid the cab driver off at Seventh and Spring. We walked one block over to Main Street, and then up in the direction of the Pacific Electric station. If either cab driver was later questioned, there was little information he could give.

Main Street was full of bums and no one paid attention to the way I carried my coat. But I had the feeling that a thousand pairs of eyes watched. I was full of fear, and I hated myself for it. I wanted to give up. I wanted to die right here. I was so scared I thought I'd vomit. The fear was in my stomach going every direction. My teeth ached. I was disgusted with myself. The handcuffs hurt my wrists. *It must be perfectly obvious that I'm wearing handcuffs.* It was only Jill here beside me that made me keep on. I must have been a spectacle. I hadn't been nearly this scared when they arrested me.

113

In the station Jill went to the information booth and I sat down on a waiting room bench. I felt desolated. It was hot in the station, and there was sweat on my face, but I was shivering. I tried to watch advertising slides on a little screen in front of me. A kid at my side, holding a greasy bag of popcorn, was hopping up and down. There was the sound of endless shoes on the dirty tile floor. The hands on the big clock inside the station were semaphored at twenty minutes to eight. A train was being called. Now I saw Jill. I saw the neat green sandals with the red cork heels, and my eyes came up.

She had tickets in her hand. I rose and followed her. We were going toward a gate that was already open. It was marked: *San Pedro*. Uniformed sailors were streaming through to the train platform. There were a few civilians.

"It's an interurban . . . leaving right away," Jill said.

"Do you see any cops?"

"No."

"We've got to be careful," I said.

What's the matter with me? I was going to pieces. If only she'd let them hang me!

I couldn't use my hands and I was clumsy getting on the car. We moved down an aisle. We found a seat, and I took the side by the window. The coat looked all right now, sitting in my lap. I watched everybody that came in. Then the train began to move.

It crawled down the big wooden trestle and turned right, and then left. Out of the window I saw trucks and horse-drawn carts. The sailors were reading newspapers, eating peanuts, talking and laughing. The conductor came and I didn't look up. Jill handed him the tickets. He punched them and gave them back.

The car got out of town. It left the suburbs behind and thundered down the tracks. I could see stars in the sky, and the moon was thin and white.

Chapter Eighteen

We took a room in a shabby hotel in San Pedro. The proprietress was an old woman and she showed no particular interest in the transaction. The room was musty and the wallpaper was stained where rain had dripped down from the roof, but it had the air of cleanliness, with a big old-fashioned bed and a worn brown carpet. From the window it was possible to see the harbor and part of the Wilmington trestle, and an old marine yard where several ships were junked. Now and then a freighter went out through the channel and you heard its big bass horn. There were a great many seagulls that squawked and screamed, and the air was crisp and cold. It tasted of salt.

Jill had no trouble in picking the lock of the handcuffs and when they were off, I rubbed my wrists for a very long time, and stretched my arms out. I felt much better, and I could think better. There had been no time for Jill to get a coat and I put mine over her shoulders. She smiled up at me, and I kissed her, and walked over to the window. I stood there for a long time watching the harbor.

"You'll catch cold, darling."

"Nonsense," I said. "Do you think we're safe here?"

"Of course. And tomorrow we'll get a room with a fire escape. Quick exit."

"I can just see that. Me with my pants in one hand and my shoes in the other. You in your silk undies. Nymphs in the night."

"And, darling, think how mortified I'd be if you were shot when you didn't have your pants on!"

"It's ghastly," I said. "I can even see the headlines. *Pantless killer and shameless woman lie side by side in the San Pedro morgue.*"

"Darling, am I shameless?"

"Well, you ain't honest, Miss Lynn. Think what the W.C.T.U. would say."

"I don't care! We'll get married when it's over, Peg, when they arrest the real killer."

"Heh. Heh. Why? To give our grandchildren a name?"

"Don't be so pessimistic. They'll get the killer all right."

"Oh, sure! They start a man hunt for us—and find him instead. Just like on Peter Gunn."

"Well, anyhow, Peg, I'll be your wife. Or at least your mistress. Every writer should have a mistress, you know."

"That's a thought. I'll take it up with the Writers' Guild. For every writer a mistress. It should boom things."

"We're going to have fine times, aren't we, darling?"

"Oh, we'll have lovely times, all right! Hiding like criminals! Probably starving! Running away from cops . . . Christ!"

My coat was over her shoulders, but she was shivering. The room was damp.

"We'll just—forget the cops," she said.

"You're awfully good to me, Jill. Come on, let's go to bed. We'll forget the damn cops all right!"

In the morning the winter sun was feeble on the windows; the harbor was the color of slate, and very choppy, flecked with white froth. The room reeked with an old wooden smell. There was no activity in the rusty marine yard and very few people on the street in this end of town. Jill had dressed and gone out. She came in with a tray covered by a napkin and I sat up in bed. I needed a shave. But the winter morning felt good and the surroundings were strange and pleasant. It was exactly like your first morning in a foreign country. Everything was new and you did not mind the hardship. It occurred to me that I was perhaps almost happy. Jill sat down on the bed opposite me, breaking her eggs in a cup.

"This is a quite wonderful breakfast," I said. "Where did you get it?"

"There's a Greasy Spoon about a block from here."

I smiled at her with a mouthful of toast. "It was thoughtful of you to mention the name of the place. It sharpens my appetite." I swallowed. "How much did it come to?"

"Sixty-five cents. It leaves us a total balance of $47.52."

"Spoken like an adding machine!"

She grinned, sipping her coffee. But she looked worried.

"What's the matter, Jill?"

"Nothing," she said. "I guess I'm a little upset. I think we'd better move to that other room. The one with the fire escape."

"I remember—the one with the pants. But why?"

She handed me the morning paper. I glanced at the headlines.

"Hey—this is swell!"

"What's swell?"

"My name in big type like this," I said. "For a writer used to by-lines it's a very interesting study. It was never like this in *Cosmopolitan!*"

"Darling, would you mind very much sobering up?"

"What do you know about it! Have you ever gone to sleep dreaming of your name in big letters? No! Have you ever rushed to a newsstand when you had a serial beginning only to discover the whole cover had been given to a short story by Sloan Wilson? No! This—this is memorial!"

"It may be immemorial. Do you realize half the state is looking for us?"

I glared down at the paper again.

"That's a very bad picture. I like the one of you much better."

"Peg!"

"Yes?"

"What are we going to do?"

"I asked you that last night. You said we'd just be careful of the police."

"I know. I was very wise last night and very clever. Today it's different. I'm *scared*, Peg!"

"I'm glad we have that emotion at separate times."

"You aren't scared today?"

"Well, I wasn't. I was just thinking how nice the harbor looked. I forgot I was me. I was having a fine time being somebody else."

I finished the breakfast and sipped my coffee and read the paper. Ed Cornell had recovered all right. He'd have me in custody before nightfall. It was a dirty trick I had played on him, and he didn't mean to let it go. Much was made of the fact that I was on contract to a studio. *Moom pitchers* had landed smack on the front page with the publicity they had so much wanted to avoid.

"I remember when they were looking for that hitchhiker killer," Jill said. "They had everybody out. Even boy scouts going through the woods beating drums. Every man on the street his size or description was stopped. If he didn't stop he was shot."

"Did they finally get him?"

"Yes. In Washington. A State Trooper made the arrest. Everybody was incensed and that hitchhiker killer was executed right away."

"But *I'm* not—"

"To people who read the papers it's almost the same, don't you see?"

"Yes."

"The fact that you've run away is proof enough to the public of your guilt."

"I suppose so. But I wouldn't have had a chance in court and—"

"Of course not! But a man hunt makes very good reading. The police will be on their toes."

I pushed the paper away.

"What are you going to do?"

"Get dressed."

"We'd better not leave here until dark," she said.

"Do you think it's that bad?"

"I know it is. The papers said fugitives come to the harbor —hoping to get a ship going out."

"That's a thought."

"No, it isn't. All the ships will be watched."

"Are you sorry you came with me?"

She looked up. "No, darling. You know I'm not! I'm just worried, that's all!"

A white gull drifted down over the gray harbor. A freighter was coming in.

The darkness came at five, and at six we left the hotel. The day had been very long, and we had not eaten since breakfast. They say your stomach is a nerve center. I had a small burning pain in my stomach but I did not know then that it was serious. We had decided my tan coat would have been too conspicuous and we left it behind in the room. The street was dark with lamp posts only at the corners. There was a stiff, cold wind from the harbor. Now that we were outside the old fear came back.

We walked into town. The lights of the stores were frightening at first and we kept our eyes down and did not look at the people we passed. But they were mostly sailors, some in uniform, others in woolen sweaters and dungarees, off freighters and tankers. There were a number of women. The women did not wear slacks like they do in Hollywood. They wore gingham dresses and cheap silk and rayon. Most of the young ones were with navy men, and I did not see any that were good looking. But I imagine that beauty in a woman is only a way you get of thinking. Jill was shapely and handsome and a few sailors turned around, the way you'd turn around if you saw a million dollars.

There were no policemen, except those directing traffic, and after a while I became very brave and went into a cheap drygoods store and bought a sweat shirt. Jill waited outside and I bought a sweater for her. I put the sweat shirt on there in the store, and brought the sweater out to her. These garments did not very much change the descriptions of our clothes that had been broadcast, but they put us in a garb that fit the background. There was a stubble of beard on my face, and that also helped, or I hoped that it would.

We crossed the street, past the interurban station, and walked over the railroad tracks down to the old Fifth Street Landing. The major units of the fleet were in Hawaii and a few idle shore boats were tied up. There was a big sign that read *Water Taxis to the Warships—25¢*. Nearby there was a hamburger stand. It was doing no business at all and the man behind the counter sat in the dim light reading the sports page of a newspaper. There were all kinds of bugs around the light and some of them stuck on the globe. But the black skillet looked clean and hot and Jill and I sat down on stools. My stomach still bothered me, and I imagined it was only because I was hungry.

We ordered bowls of chile con carne and hamburger steak on a plate with two fried eggs each. We ate ravenously and drank lukewarm coffee to wash it down. But I sat with my stool turned a little to one side so I could see if anybody came. Two railroad trackmen went by and each time I got rigid.

After we had started to eat the counterman turned on a dinky radio. He leaned on the counter and began talking about football. He was very much concerned about the Rose Bowl game. I kept saying "Yeah," and "You're certainly right about that," and once Jill said: "We saw USC play Washington." This was very bad because he immediately wanted to know all about USC. He began naming players. The first thing I knew we were going over the fine points of the Notre Dame game, and then he began talking about Red Sanders. "There was a coach," he said.

He would not stop talking and I was suddenly trying to listen through his voice to the seven o'clock news. I could get whole chunks about the international situation. But when it became local the counter man was shaking a pancake turner in my face. He remembered Bob Waterfield when he played for UCLA. The home games had always been in the Coliseum, and in Waterfield's senior year, he hadn't missed a single one of them. "And now he's the coach of the Rams."

Just as he said that I heard my name on the radio. I lost all of what followed until the announcer said: "*Jill Lynn, who is with the fugitive, will be charged with—*" then UCLA, and after that: "*—posted a five thousand dollar reward for the pair. Mr. Cornell, active as a homicide detective for a number of years—*"

"I tell you they don't have games like that any more."

"No, I guess not."

The news went off. There was a station announcement, then the theme of a dance band came on.

When we walked off the band was playing the theme from *Mr. Lucky.* There was the sound of a boat motor starting up.

"Let's go for a ride."

"Where to?"

"I don't know."

"We can't afford it," she said.

"We've got forty-four dollars left."

"Then we can't afford anything, darling, let alone a boat ride."

"How was the hamburger steak?"

"It was fine," she said, "it really was."

"Did you hear the news?"

"I got a little of it."

"There's a reward."

"Yes, I heard that part."

"Somehow I don't care."

"You don't?"

"No. If we last as long as Jean Valjean did in *Les Miserables,* we'll have lovely times—and ten children. It's different living together, isn't it? It's different and better."

"It's swell, Peg. I think Vicky'd be glad if she knew."

We were walking across the tracks. There was a three-car interurban waiting at the station. The windows in the big red cars were lighted up but there were no passengers inside. I began thinking of Vicky—and the murder. Lanny could have done it, of course. With all his weeping and hysteria he was capable of rage. And Hurd Evans with his slave bracelet. *They had never discovered the instrument of crime!* My thoughts were vague and jumbled. There was Robin Ray—something about a crack-up in his car, a minor accident. . . . Harry Williams was dead, of course. He'd gotten in the killer's way. There'd been two murders—only one on the books. This was the way my thoughts ran, getting nowhere. . . .

Jill and I crossed the street and walked up a block. There was a bus going by, and a lot of traffic. I saw the marquee of a movie theater, and the big brick police station which is on the hill overlooking the harbor. We went the other way, searching for a hotel that looked old enough to be safe. We passed the Seaman's Institute and several pool rooms. There were quite a few Filipinos on the street. Once I saw three of them drive by in a car with a pimply prostitute blonde. I already had indigestion and suddenly I felt terrible. I was not used to walking so much and my legs ached. I felt weak all over.

"I've got a stomach-ache."

"No!"

"It feels a little like appendicitis."

"Where is the pain?"

"Just in my stomach. It burns."

"We'd better get a room."

"Yes, I think we should."

"We'll find one right away," Jill said.

We walked up a very dark street. There were old buildings on it and a big, gaudy clothing and jewelry store that displayed a sign *Credit to Navy Men*. It was closed down and was dark.

I didn't see the man who stood in the doorway until he stepped out. He was big and heavy set. "Got a match, buddy?" he said. Then I saw the way he was looking at us, trying to make sure.

He was a cop!

Chapter Nineteen

It was quite dark here, but he must have decided that we were the McCoy because I saw him go for his gun. I didn't wait. I hit him. I don't know where I got the strength. I think it was the sudden awful panic. The guy's head jolted back and hit the window. I thought I heard the glass crack. Jill and I were running. I don't know how we could run. I heard the detective shout, then we were around the corner. We kept running. We brushed past people. Everything went black in my head but my legs were still running.

By this time the cop was around the corner. I thought probably he'd start shooting. There was an apartment house opposite us—Jill and I dashed in through the front hall. The cop had seen us! We raced for the back exit. But I saw an apartment door ajar—as though someone had gone out without closing it securely. For a second Jill and I stood there in the dimly lit corridor. She looked at me, and I nodded. I opened the door, and we slipped into the apartment.

There was a draft and the half open door banged shut. The sound froze us up.

"Is that you, Henry?" A woman's voice from another room.

We were in a dank little living room. There was a lamp on the reading table, and a portable radio. I heard the sound of splashing water. The woman was in the bathtub! Jill turned back to the door. Footsteps sounded harshly in the hall. The cop!

"Henry—is that you?"

"Say *something*," Jill whispered.

"You say it. Say there's nobody here but us chickens."

"Henry!"

"Yeah?" I said. I muffled my voice.

"It took you long enough to answer. Did you bring the eggs?"

"Yeah—"

Jill turned on the radio. Dance music flooded into the room. It helped disguise whatever there was left of my voice.

"You were certainly gone long enough," the woman in the bathroom said.

"My God!" said Jill. *"Henry must already be overdue!"*

"That's nice! The detective's out there in the hall phoning for a radio car!"

Jill and I both saw the divan at the same time. It had a tall back, and we could probably hide there and wait awhile. There was a window nearby, and if the cops did come in here we could make a break that way. We started for the divan. Just then there was the sound of a key in the lock of the hall door. I don't know yet how we did it. It was not ours to reason why! But when Henry walked in, a lanky longshoreman, a bag of eggs in his big hand, we were out of sight.

"I say, Henry—must you play the radio so loud?" She was splashing.

Henry rubbed his lean jaw, walked over and turned off the radio. "If you didn't want it—what the hell'd you turn it on for?"

"I? Me?"

"Yes, you. Who do you think I'm talking to?"

123

"Are you saying *I* turned on the radio?"

"I know God-damned well I didn't!"

"Well, who did?"

"Go on, you Irish bitch, tell me it was the fairies! Go ahead, say it was fairies that done it!"

"Henry, you yourself turned it on this minute. What are you talking about?" She splashed furiously.

He stood in the middle of the room, yelling. "You're the funniest woman I ever saw. A man never knows what you're going to say next!"

"*You* never know what *I'm* going to say next? I ask you a civil question—such as did you bring the eggs, and what kind of an answer do I get? *Yeah.* You mumble *yeah!* You talk like you've got a mouthful of oysters. All you ever eat. Oysters!"

"I mumble *yeah?*"

"Henry—don't try and tell me—" It sounded as though she were climbing out of the tub. The bathroom door was open, and he went in.

"We'd better get out," Jill whispered.

"Can't—he'd see us!"

I was holding my stomach. I was sick as a dog. The pain stabbed and wrenched at me. *"A fine place to have appendicitis,"* I said. *"You must try having appendicitis behind a divan sometime."*

The woman had one leg up on the bathtub and was wiping herself with a towel. She was about thirty-five but she had a good, round figure. Her hair was grayish-brown and she had it tight in a knot. Her buttocks moved like jelly as she rubbed herself with the towel.

"You're a crazy damn woman, aren't you?" Henry said.

"I distinctly heard you say *yeah.*"

"You're just crazy, aren't you?"

"I distinctly—"

"You're crazy, but you're—nice."

"Henry—"

He picked her up and carried her into the living room. I heard her body thump solidly as he laid her on the divan.

I looked at Jill. We were crouched way down. Only the pain in my guts was so bad I didn't give a damn. Jill's face was scarlet. Now there was a loud knocking on the door.

"Henry, dear . . ."

"God damn it!" Henry said.

The third time the knock sounded Henry got up. In a moment he started for the door. The woman rose and fled for the bedroom. Henry yanked the hall door.

"Well?"

"It's the police . . . we're looking for a man and a woman who—"

"There's nobody here!"

"Are you sure?"

"Damn right I'm sure. Has a man no privacy! Can't a man—"

"All right. Sorry we had to bother you."

Henry slammed the door. He rubbed his chin again. His eyes were glazed. Now he started for the bedroom.

The bedroom door closed.

I could scarcely get to my feet. I wanted to bend over double with the pain in my stomach. I got to the window and pried it open. I lifted Jill out, lowered her to the ground. I jumped down beside her.

It was very dark, and there was a mist from the harbor. We crept along the side of the building to the street. I didn't know if I could stand up much longer. A patrol car stood in front of the apartment house, but it was empty. I kept my hand on my stomach. It was hard for me to breathe. On the nearest corner there was a taxi. Jill and I plunged out from the side of the building and made a run for it. Running—I thought I'd tear my insides out. The taxi was a big and very old Cadillac. When I was inside, on the back seat, I almost passed out. I was only half conscious.

Jill was leaning forward and shaking somebody. It was the cab's driver. His car was parked and he'd been dozing behind the wheel. I remember seeing Jill shake him. Then the car started. I was doubled up in the seat. Jill was saying:

"Yes, the tourist camp will be fine. Dear, he says there's a tourist camp just three miles from here."

"I take calls there all the time," said the driver. "There's never any trouble."

"Do you get a commission?" Jill asked.

I was doubled up and holding my stomach. Pains were shooting from it and going all through me.

"Well, I get a little," the driver admitted. He was a Portugee.

"That's all right," Jill said. "We don't mind. Do we, dear?"

"No," I said.

"I suppose you'd even register for us," said Jill.

"Sure, I'll do that," the driver said.

"You know how it is," Jill said. "Sometimes it is very embarrassing."

"I can understand that," said the driver. "I will be glad to be of service."

"You are very considerate."

"I'm not considerate at all. It's only what I'd do for any couple who'd rather have it that way."

"Well, we *would* rather have it that way, wouldn't we, dear?"

"Yes," I said.

"These tourist cabins are near Long Beach," the driver said. "They are comfortable and you will like them."

"I'm sure we will," said Jill. She was looking out through the back window.

"Are we being followed?" I whispered.

"No."

"Did they chase?"

"Did you say something?" the driver asked.

"We were just talking among ourselves back here."

"Oh, I beg your pardon."

"It's quite all right."

"I was sound asleep when you woke me," said the driver. "I'm much better now."

We were on the road for Long Beach and there were oil wells, and some big tanks, and the smell of oil, and the smell of the ocean. The winter stars were very dim and there was no moon. I wanted to vomit, but I held it back. I couldn't be still. I kept moving from side to side.

The tourist cabin was dirty and the light was dim, but the sheets were clean and I took off my clothes and got into bed. The driver had brought the key of the cabin to us. He said he had registered and that we were Mr. and Mrs. Thompson. He said everybody liked the name Thompson, and he always used it. Jill sent him back for a pitcher of cracked ice and when he returned he collected for the cabin. He said the price was five dollars. Jill was almost sick and she no longer thought she had been so smart. But I paid him and got rid of him.

"That's an awful price."

"Not under the circumstances."

"I hate his filthy mind," Jill said.

"His filthy mind came in very handy. We didn't have to risk registering," I said. "Do you think he'd suspect us?"

"No, darling. He's apparently used to this and I don't believe any other thought will cross his little brain. Besides, he was half asleep."

"I hope so," I said.

"He was, really."

"If he tells the cops he brought us here," I said, "we're cooked."

She locked the door and propped a chair against it, the back of the chair up under the knob. I was crawling into bed.

"How do you feel?"

"No better. I'm glad you thought of asking him for ice."

"Yes, I thought you might need it. We had a close scrape with that policeman, didn't we?"

"Very close."

"Shall I make you an ice pack?"

"That'd be swell. Use a face towel and wrap the ice up in it. That Henry was a card, wasn't he?"

"He was a beast!"

"*Jesus!*"

"Is the pain getting worse?"

"Yes, all the time."

"Darling, you look dreadful. Like—like an oyster!"

"That's the way I feel."

"You're very white. Do you think it's really appendicitis?"

"Yes."

"Then we'd better call a doctor."

"No. Just get the ice."

"All right. You frighten me."

"Don't be frightened," I said.

She made a very good ice pack and I lay back on the pillow and let it freeze my side. I did not feel cold where the ice touched me but numb. I no longer had nausea, and the pain was no worse. Jill put her hand on my forehead and she said I was very hot. I wanted to move around but I lay very still with the ice pack on my side. There was no lamp but Jill turned off the main light and left the light on in the bathroom and the bathroom door open. Then she pulled up a chair, and sat in the semi-darkness and stroked my head.

I didn't remember going to sleep but when I opened my eyes Jill was still there. I was wearing a fresh ice pack and the pain was much worse. I was seized with a convulsing nausea.

"How long was I asleep?"

"Almost four hours."

"I can't believe it. I—"

I got up out of bed and went into the bathroom. I was very sick in the bathroom. In the next hour I went there a number of times and was sick. Then I lay on the bed and turned from side to side. I was covered with sweat. There was no more ice. The sweat kept rolling off my body.

"You look ghastly, Peg. I'm going to call a doctor."

"No."

"But you have acute appendicitis!"

"Don't call a doctor. I couldn't stand to have this end that way. What rotten luck!"

"How are you now?"

"I'm better," I lied.

"Tell me the truth."

"I am. I'm a little better."

"Your appendix might burst, you know,"

"Not now. It's getting better."

"You'd die if it burst."

"Would I go to hell, mommy?"

128

"Yes, darling. A very special hell. Can't you lie still? It must be awful if you can't lie still."

"Sure, I can lie still."

"You're making yourself do it!"

"No, I'm not."

"Oh, darling!"

"You're very good to me, Jill."

"I wish I had the pain."

"Don't wish that."

"Isn't there something I can do for you?"

"No—nothing."

"If I got a doctor he *might* not be suspicious."

"No. He'd have to turn in a report. Then they'd—you know what they'd do."

"Yes, I know what they'd do! You precious sweet, it's so—"

"They'd lock you up, too," I said.

"It doesn't matter about me."

"Yes, it does."

"Darling, you're rigid!"

"I'm trying to lie still," I said. "*Jesus—*"

"Is the pain awful?"

"No—it's—I'll be all right in a minute—*oh, Jesus God!*"

"Peg, are you—"

"No—I'll be—okay."

(*I will be, won't I?*)

"Is it all right if I move a little bit?"

"You poor darling, the pain is worse, isn't it?"

"No. I just want to change my position."

"I'm going to get a doctor."

"No. Stay close to me. Please stay close to me, *Jill—*"

"I'm right here, darling."

"Keep hold of my hand."

"You're very weak," she said.

"I'm tired."

"Try and go to sleep. Keep your eyes closed."

I kept my eyes closed and the pain was just as bad. She stroked my head. I was thoroughly exhausted and there was a sour taste in my mouth and my throat burned. I could taste the hamburger and the chile. I did not open my eyes and after a long time I was so tired I could not stay awake.

When I woke the sky was a dirty gray and there was the smell of oil wells, and very far away I heard a boat whistle. Jill sat on the chair holding my hand but she had dozed off. I felt very shaky and hollow but the pain was gone. Either your appendix bursts or it doesn't. If it doesn't, the attack subsides. The sour taste was still in my mouth and the sheets on the bed were wet with sweat. I reached for a cigarette. My hands trembled as I lit it. It felt good to smoke. I thought I must need a shave very badly. I looked at Jill. She was nodding, her head on her chest. I lifted her hand and kissed it.

Outside the fog was rolling in from the sea and the room was very cold.

Chapter Twenty

On that day we took a small apartment in Long Beach. I paid twenty-five dollars for two weeks' rent and a dollar deposit on the electric lights. Jill went to an open air market and came back with two large sacks of groceries. I was still very weak and I stayed in bed. The next day at a rummage sale of old clothes Jill found a corduroy skirt and a brown and white sweater for herself. For me she picked out a pair of faded dungaree trousers and a seaman's blue wool cap. She paid very little for these things and we still had twelve dollars left. Jill looked fine and full-breasted in the sweater, and the skirt was tight and lovely across her hips.

"Now no one can identify us by our clothes," she said

"Not unless they look at your shoes."

"I'm going to dye them brown."

"And your hair?"

"I'm going to leave my hair alone. Would you want me to change it, darling?"

"No," I said.

"I'll change it if you don't like it."

"No, you have lovely hair. I was only thinking of the police."

"There are so many blondes," she said, "I don't think it'd make much difference."

"No, I guess not."

"Are you hungry? What would you like for supper?"

"What have you got?"

"Lamb patties," she said. "They were twenty cents apiece."

We had a fine supper. We sat in the kitchenette, and the window was on the court. You could hear a kid wailing, and somebody's radio that was turned up too loud. The radio went from morning to night and you always heard it. When supper was over I sipped my coffee and read the evening paper. The search was going on very intensely. The police announced they had a clue and it would only be a matter of time before we were brought into custody. On the second page there was a picture of the handcuffs and the tan coat we had left behind in the San Pedro hotel. All of the old publicity photos of Vicky had been dug up and different ones were used. The reward stood at five thousand dollars. It seemed Ed Cornell was the kind of guy who had always saved his pay and it was he who had put up the dough. The papers were making quite a fuss over him.

I laid the news aside and went into the other room. I looked in the mirror at the dungarees, the sweat shirt and my beard. It was getting to be quite a beard, and tomorrow I would straighten it up with a razor and it would look legitimate. Jill came in and I turned toward her.

"Who are these people the police want?"

She laughed.

"I don't think we look like them at all," I said.

But the next morning the headlines of the local papers announced that we were believed to be in Long Beach. I felt as though an icy wind had suddenly blown over me. The Portugee cab driver had come forward with the story that he had taken a couple of our description to a tourist camp. He said it was an ordinary trip and he had suspected nothing that night, but reading the papers had made him think. The tourist cabin had been ransacked and it was thought we had proceeded from there into Long Beach.

"They aren't far behind."

"No," Jill said.

"Do you think we should go on?"

"We wouldn't have a chance," she said. "We haven't enough money; besides, they're watching all the roads."

We stayed inside all day. That night Jill went out to the dime store and bought toilet articles and a cheap deck of cards. She brought me a razor, and I trimmed up the beard. Then I sat on the bed, wearing dungaree trousers and an undershirt, and we played cards. She taught me Russian Bank. It was a fascinating game but I was very stupid and she always beat me. Outside, we could hear the traffic on the boulevard; and across the court there was dance music on the radio that was turned up too loud.

"Darling, you can play better than this. You know a ten doesn't go on a queen."

"What does go on a queen?"

"A jack," she said.

"Mm!"

"Silly!"

My mind wasn't on the cards. I was thinking about Hollywood. It seemed remote and far away; and all the time now I kept thinking of the murder. I'd remember Hollywood's tension, the feverish nights, the rotten little jealousies, the screaming ego, the petty smugness . . . and only a few sweet guys.

I'd remember Lanny Craig saying: *"They crucified me . . . it was because of Vicky Lynn!"* And the night Robin Ray said: *"She'd laugh, see, and it was like music of a Jackie Gleason album."* And Hurd Evans: *"I only get two hundred and fifty a week."* Tick-tock, the faceless clock on Sunset. *"It's possible to build a case out of nothing,"* the assistant district attorney said. Where was Harry Williams? If he'd been murdered, where was his body?

"Darling, you've made half a dozen mistakes. I don't think we'd better play any more. You're worried, aren't you, sweet?"

"No. Only I was thinking."

132

"Of what?"

"That if Ed Cornell could build up a case against me—why couldn't I do the same thing to somebody else?"

"Silly, he's a detective. He knows all about how to do it."

"Granted. But I wonder if I happen to be right? Wonder if there was one thing that would prove it beyond all shadow of doubt?"

"What is the one thing?"

"Harry Williams' corpse."

"How do you know he is a corpse?"

"I don't."

"Well?"

"I don't know," I said. "I was just going over a lot of things. I'm mixed up now. But there's got to be a solution, don't you see?"

"The police haven't figured it out."

"I know. But I'm Renfrew of the Mounted—remember?"

I lit a cigarette and got up and walked over to the window. Jill came up behind me. She had nice soft hips, and I put my hands on her hips and kissed her cheek, and her ears.

"If it wasn't for you, Jill—none of this'd matter. But—you make me want to fight."

"Darling, you can't fight the world."

"No, but I can try. The whole thing is so complex. If only I could see some ray of light through it!"

"You say you suspect Hurd or Lanny or Robin. But you aren't even sure of that."

"No. I'm not sure of anything."

"It'll work out."

I shook my head. "Nothing ever works out by itself."

We stood together at the window and were silent. The radio across the court had gone off and the night was very quiet. Yet on every street and in every avenue the police were hunting us.

By Christmas my beard was very good and I put on the dungarees and the seaman's woolen cap and a pair of green glasses and went out on the street in daylight. It was a cloudy day, almost gray, and the air was crisp and cold. Jill

133

would not let me spend money on food but I bought a little table-sized Christmas tree that had been marked down to fifteen cents, and in a drug store I got a box of tinsel for a dime.

I returned to the apartment and set the tree up. Jill made popcorn and these white puffs I hung on the small branches with strips of tinsel. It took me a long time to complete the job; when I was finished the tree was all white and silver. The early darkness had come outside, and it looked very pretty.

"Look, Jill, ain't it elegant?"

"Oh, Peg, it's beautiful! How did you ever dress it like that?"

"It's nothing, really, Miss Lynn. Take off your clothes and give me a string of popcorn and I'll do as much for you."

She laughed. "You would, too! Supper's on. And please hurry, darling. This is our Christmas dinner, you know."

She had turned off the lights in the kitchenette and lighted little five-cent candles. They were red candles and they flickered very brightly, one at my place, and one at hers. I sat down, and Jill brought the first course. It was a bowl of bread and milk on which she had sprinkled some sugar. She sat down, and I lifted my spoon, but she shook her head.

"I think on Christmas we should say grace."

"All right."

She bowed her head and folded her hands. There in the candlelight it seemed to me that she looked very lovely.

"Dear God, we thank You for the food we are about to receive. And we thank You for this, for—" She looked up. "Oh, Peg! I am thankful!" Tears splashed down her face. "You'll never know how much our love means to me!"

"Poor sweet!"

She wiped away the tears. "Merry Christmas, darling! Do you know something? This is the loveliest Christmas I've ever had!"

We ate the bread and milk and when we were finished she brought on white flakes of tuna fish which was meant to be the turkey. The tuna fish was crisp and delicious and we ate all of it. For dessert she had prepared raspberry junket. We stayed in the kitchenette drinking our coffee until very late and the radio across the court was tuned to Christmas carols. The carols sounded clear and sweet. Our candles burned down to fat red stubs and we blew them out and went into the other room.

On the third of January we ran out of money and there was not enough food left for supper. Less was printed about us in the papers these days. The only news items were those concerning gasoline station attendants who claimed they saw us. There was one in San Diego and another somewhere in Montana. They were positive we had driven in and bought gas, and if we were found in that vicinity they thought it only fair that they should receive part of the reward.

Jill and I did not talk about the food situation. We agreed that we should not appear together outside any longer, it was too dangerous. When I left that day I said I was going to try and find some kind of a job.

"Peg, be careful."

"I will. But there should be some kind of a job I could do. I'll take a walk along the waterfront."

"I can't imagine you a stevedore."

"Neither can I. They have unions. But there may be a part time job I could get."

"I doubt it."

"Well, a man can try."

She was picking at a thread on her skirt. "What time will you be back?"

"In time for—" I caught myself.

"Say it, Peg! In time for supper."

"There'll be supper," I said. "You wait and see!"

All of that morning I marched doggedly from place to place. I went into lumber yards and ship yards, and to factories. In the afternoon I was hungry and very tired. I walked along the pike. Now on a winter afternoon the amusement palaces were almost entirely shut down. The only concessions open were a few stray hot dog stands, a lonely roller coaster, and a taxi dance hall which ran matinees every afternoon and did a fine business. Sailors and longshoremen flocked to it. I stood in the doorway for a moment and watched. The dance floor was dark but crowded. The music was raucous and there was the cheap smell of hot armpits and gaudy perfume.

I left and went on in search of work. I applied everywhere along the waterfront. Sometimes I ran into queues of men waiting to fill a job, and I waited in one queue for an hour and fifteen minutes. It was at a side door of a cannery and some of the men had been here since ten o'clock. In the end a foreman came out and told us that the jobs had been taken.

It was early dusk, and past the supper hour. Jill would be waiting for me, but I was exhausted and very discouraged. I had never been quite so hungry. I walked along the beach and after a while I lay down on the sand and closed my eyes. For a moment I saw red spots and then they went away.

There was a cooling breeze from the ocean. It felt very good and I began to think of Hollywood. *Could Lanny Craig have killed Vicky?* Somehow I was unable to entertain the thought. That was the trouble with me: it was so difficult to suspect these men I had known. Robin Ray had been in love with Vicky. All right. He had admitted it. Jill had said that she was going to tell Robin—on the day that she was murdered!—that she was leaving him for me.

I suddenly sat bolt upright.

I remembered it had once been in the gossip columns that Robin was incapable of holding his women. He had been thrown over by a couple of second-rate stars and it embarrassed him very much. Besides, in the hands of gossips, it was bad publicity. He played virile rôles and it cast a reflection on his manhood. If it happened again—spectacularly enough—it could hurt his career. His career was somewhat rocky anyway. *"Let's face it, old man. My rôles are getting worse. My option's running short."*

That was established. Robin could not afford to be publicly jilted by another woman. It was ridiculous, but there it was. And tons of publicity had linked Robin's name with Vicky's. Supposing she had told him on the day of the murder that she was going to leave him! What if they had ar-

136

gued about it—violently! First because he actually loved her, and second because his career couldn't stand having her leave him. What if they had argued and—

I was on my feet.

I recalled that day in the commissary we had first discussed promoting Vicky. There had been a big, shiny ring on Robin's finger. He wore it constantly: yet I hadn't seen it since the day of the murder! If he had hit her wearing that ring, had struck her on the side of the head—

I paused. Could this have happened in his car?

I started back to the apartment. Yes, *that was it!* In his car. He had picked her up on Sunset after she signed the contract. They could have argued and in a wild rage he could have hit her. Perhaps he hadn't meant to.

I could scarcely get my breath. All of the scattered thoughts that had been in my mind were falling together and I was beginning to see the picture they made. Now one more link dropped into place.

"I'll drink to the dope that put a new windshield in my car and didn't make it shatter-proof glass. I'll drink to him."

"Did you break your windshield?" I had said.

"Yes, that was about a month ago."

The murder had been committed a month before he said that! What a fool I'd been not to see it!

Yet, if there were anything to this suspicion, if he had killed her in the car—how was it she had been found in the apartment?

I thought it out slowly. There could have been the argument in the car. He had lost his temper and hit her. In the excitement he had let go of the wheel and swerved into another car or against the curb, with such a crash that the windshield had shattered.

He got control of himself then and drove away from the scene of the accident. Vicky was unconscious or dead from his blow. But at this point he couldn't have possibly known that she was dead or going to die. He wouldn't have realized that he had hit her that hard. His only thought was to get her home.

He had parked the car at the side entrance of the apartment and carried her in through the door and up the back

137

steps. If by this time he realized she was dead, it was too late to change his course. He must have been terrified!

He had to get her into the apartment somehow and he must have searched her purse for the key. He wouldn't have found it. She had given it to me. What had he done? There was a fire escape on that side of the building and he could have taken her out on that and in through the windows.

The fire escape windows had been open when I found Vicky's body!

Robin must have left her there on the floor and gone in to the hall. But Harry Williams had been coming down the hall, just the way Ed Cornell had described it, and Robin had run into him. Robin had been in the position Cornell had charged me with facing. And Robin had consequently taken care of Harry Williams!

It was complete now. Complete! I was half running to get back to the apartment.

How could I prove it! How could I possibly prove these things?

I didn't know. I wanted to talk to Jill about it. Pieced together it all seemed amazingly clear. There were certain points: the ring, the shattered windshield, and the motive—on which I couldn't possibly be wrong.

The apartment was several blocks from the waterfront and I was already out of breath. I was getting that hot pain you get in your side when you run. The street was crowded with people, and I brushed past them. Old ladies with bundles; guys taking their girls to the movies; kids selling papers. Trucks went by, and the local busses, their lights shining in the night. You could hear a traffic cop's whistle, and the clanging bell as a signal light changed. No one seemed excited. No one noticed me. I was late getting back. Jill would be worried. She'd he terribly worried. I had been gone all day. I was suddenly glad I had someone to whom I could pour out these things. There were less people on the street now. I was nearly there.

That last block was awful. Then I came in through the little courts and to the door of the one which belonged to us. I unlocked it and went in. The room was empty. I glanced toward the kitchenette. There was no one in it.

"Jill," I said. I was suddenly scared. *"Jill!"*
There was no answer.

Chapter Twenty-One

I must have gone a little crazy. I went into the kitchenette and shouted her name. I walked all around the apartment. I was shaking. I'd never felt an emotion like this. It was a hell of a lot more than fear. I haven't any word for it. I thought I was going to start crying. I didn't know what to do. I fumbled in my pocket for a cigarette. There weren't any. We'd run out of cigarettes as well as food. I searched all my pockets. Then I picked up a butt from an ash tray and held it between my fingers and lit it. It had a bad taste.

The apartment was so damned empty! I tried to think. Where was she? Now I saw something on the chair. I walked over and looked at it. It was her corduroy skirt and brown and white sweater. On the floor there was a little wad of tinfoil. I didn't know where the tinfoil had come from. I rushed to the closet and opened it. The green dress was gone. She was wearing her good dress. Perhaps she'd left me! Maybe she was sick of all this!

No!

I couldn't believe it. I sat down in a chair and pinched out the cigarette butt, and sucked for my breath. I didn't know what to do. My damn teeth were aching. What *should* I do? I wanted to go out and search the streets for her. But Long Beach was a big town. I wouldn't have had a chance that way. I couldn't think about Robin Ray. I didn't care about that any more. Jill was the only thing in the world that mattered.

I sat as though I were made of stone. The wind rustled the curtains at the window, and the radio across the court was going. *That damned radio!* Perhaps Jill had gotten a job. Maybe she had landed a temporary position as a clerk in a store; or in some small shop. Sure, that was it! I felt relieved. I got up and paced the room. I looked around for another butt but there were no more. Or else they were all so little you couldn't get them lighted.

Maybe Jill was at the taxi dance trying to make money for us. *The little fool! Would she do that! A thing like that!* It was possible. Of course it was! Anything was possible.

Only, Dear God, don't have it that anything happened to her. I'll do anything you say, God, only make Jill safe. Don't let the cops get her, God! Don't let that happen. I'll go to church every Sunday if you want, but don't let the cops get Jill!

She was at the taxi dance. That was it. Poor sweet kid, she'd be back any time now. We would have fun when she got back. It wouldn't even matter if we didn't eat. Just so she was here. We'd have fun. Just being together and laughing together. There was no night with Jill and no darkness. You can love a woman and it's like that. I loved everything about her. I loved her soul and I loved her body. She'd come in and I'd laugh. I'd say, "Hello, honey. Gee, you look swell, honey!"

I sat down on the bed, and laid the cards out in a game of solitaire. But I couldn't play. I was all shot. It was getting later. *My God, where was she?* I got up and went to the window. I watched through the window and I could look out through the court and see the street. *Where in the hell are you, Jill!*

Why didn't she come home? I didn't want her working in any taxi dance hall. Dancing with those guys and rubbing up against them and breathing that rotten perfume. I didn't even want her clerking in a store. Or a market. If there was any money to be made I'd make it.

I could stand it no longer and I left the apartment and went out on the street where I could see her when she came home. The main avenue was a quarter of a block up and this street was dark and empty. I leaned against a big palm tree. I was still groping around in my empty pockets for a cigarette.

I stood there very quietly against the tree. I don't know how long I was there. Suddenly I was aware that a car had slid up to the curb and stopped. It was a radio patrol car!

The cops in it didn't see me there in the dark. They were staring into the court. My heart began to hammer. I was going to pieces. *Why were they here? What were they doing here?* I was sick.

140

The cops were looking into the court. Sitting in the car and peering from the window. They didn't even glance my way. I began to make out what they were saying.

"See anything?"

"No. This is a pain in the neck—having to check back here every hour."

"Yeah."

"They had a detective in there until six o'clock. If he was coming back he'd have been back before then."

"Sure."

"Like the girl said—he must have shipped aboard that foreign tanker that left last night."

"Yeah. He was the kind of a heel that'd do that—take a powder on the girl. All those guys are the same. I wish to hell I could get my hands on the son of a bitch just once!"

"Say—"

"Yeah?"

"Wait a minute. The lights are on in that apartment!"

The other stared into the court.

"He must have come back. *Come on,* let's get going!"

They piled out of the car and rushed into the court. Sweat was rolling off my body and for a moment I couldn't move. *Jill's arrested! Jill's arrested!* I heard it over and over. I couldn't stop hearing it. It was a screaming that echoed in my head. *Jill's arrested. The cops got her! They got her! They got her!*

The cops were breaking into the apartment.

I began to run. I ran up the street, cut through back yards. I ran down another street, then I got into an alley. In the alley I stopped running.

I walked. I walked along the dark streets and on the bright ones and I didn't care who saw me. I walked through the park on Ocean Avenue and sat under the city lights and I saw tramps sleeping on benches and lovers walking by. The lovers were talking very low. Once I saw a couple kiss. They stood and kissed as though nothing else mattered. I left there and walked along the pike. In a big wire trash barrel I found a newspaper. I took the newspaper over under the lights on the roller coaster platform and read it.

The headlines were big and black. Jill Lynn arrested.

141

Police close in on fugitive hide-out. The paper said I had deserted Jill last night and gone to sea on a tanker bound for Brazil.

I read all the details carefully. The police had worked on the theory that we were somewhere in Long Beach. First they had painstakingly checked all recent hotel registrations. This job alone had taken almost three days. After that they had begun checking up on all the tenants who had rented an apartment since the day we had left the tourist camp. They had third-class detectives all over town doing this and in the course of the survey one of them had come to our apartment on the court.

A young detective had arrived there at noon today and asked Jill to identify herself. The paper said it had been several minutes before he realized that she was actually Jill Lynn! He had been ringing doorbells and questioning people all day, and he had very nearly passed Jill by when he found her.

Jill had been calm. The paper reported her only emotion had been one of bitterness. The money had run out and I had left her. *The woman scorned.* She was apparently ready to talk and tell anything she could to bring about my apprehension. They played that up big. It had a familiar ring to it; and they repeated all of the old police phrases to the effect that there is never any escape from the law.

Jill was taken into custody and afterward returned to the apartment by Los Angeles detectives and questioned. She was cool; she didn't once break down. A matron was brought in and Jill was permitted to change into her green dress. She was then taken to Los Angeles where she was booked and lodged in the city jail. She was to be charged with aiding the escape of a fugitive from justice, and assault *with intent to kill* on an officer of the law!

That was Ed Cornell's touch. He knew as well as I did that she hadn't intended to kill him!

There were pictures of the corduroy skirt and the brown and white sweater which were of no material value in the case and had been left for the photographers. *The tinfoil I'd seen had been from an exploded flashlight bulb!*

The whole business had been conducted very quietly and

even the people in the court were unaware that anything had happened. The address of the apartment was not revealed on the grounds that I might return and a crowd of curious people out in front would frighten me off. A detective had remained in the apartment until after six o'clock and now radio police were keeping a close watch on the place. In spite of this it was generally believed that I was at sea. The watch on the apartment was maintained only as a safeguard against the possibility that Jill's story had been untrue.

How close I had come! If I'd returned a half an hour earlier I'd have been arrested!

I skipped over all of the rest. It didn't matter. She had lied to protect me. She had kept her head and put on a wonderful show. All for me! She had done everything she could. It would be terribly hard on her when they discovered the truth, but she mustn't have cared. Her only concern had been for my safety!

I thought of Ed Cornell. The way he had watched me. The way he had tormented me for weeks. I had been his obsession. Now he was spewing his bitterness and his hatred on Jill. Assault—*with intent to kill!*

"You dirty bastard," I said. "I'll dedicate a book to you sometime."

I dropped the paper. I began to walk. I was cold with hatred. I was scarcely conscious of anything else. I shivered in the dungarees and the sweat shirt and the wool cap. I was going to Los Angeles. I was going to steal a car from a parking lot and go to Los Angeles.

I had parked the stolen car and for a long time I stood there on the hill and watched Robin Ray's house. I had been here on parties and I knew the layout of the rooms. But I studied it very carefully and made my plans. All of the lights had gone out an hour ago. These were the hills over the Cahuenga Pass and you could hear a coyote very far away, and the nervous flutter of night birds, and the singing crickets. It was a two-story house constructed of stone.

I moved silently across the road and my shadow was pale in the moonlight. I reached the side of the house and began to climb up along the stones. I made no sound at all. When I was at the window I slashed down at the screen with a jagged piece of rock. It tore and I jammed my fist in and unlatched it.

I crawled through the window into the room Robin was stirring on the bed. I grabbed the floor lamp and put it directly over him, so it would show down on his face. He was waking up. I switched the lamp on. He opened his eyes and blinked.

"Don't move," I said.

"Wh-what?"

"If you move I'll kill you!"

Chapter Twenty-Two

He sat there on the bed, up on one elbow, trying to penetrate the blinding light. I was on my haunches on the other side of the lamp. My whole body was rigid. I was shaking with rage.

"Who is it?" he said.

I told him.

It was half a minute before it hit him. Then he was wide awake, trying to look past the light and into the darkness at me. Robin was washed out. His eyes were bloodshot. I had an idea he'd been drinking earlier. His skin was sallow without make-up, but he was still good looking.

"Mind if I light a cigarette, old man?" he said.

"You won't need one."

He was motionless.

"I'm going to ask some questions," I said. I was talking slowly, and very low.

"Sure. Go ahead."

"I want the answers, Robin. All of them!"

"Sure."

He was rubbing his mottled skin. Apparently he was able to see me now. He could see the beard and he could see my eyes.

"That day of the murder," I said, "you picked up Vicky

Lynn outside her agent's office on the Sunset Strip."

"That's right."

"How come you never told the police?"

"I didn't at first because I figured it would have put me under suspicion, and it would have."

"What do you mean by *at first?*"

"They found out later," he said, "and I admitted it."

"Who found out?"

"Ed Cornell."

I was jarred. "Then you told him?"

"I didn't have to tell him—*I wish you'd let me have a cigarette!*—he found out by himself. You see, Vicky and I had an argument."

"About her leaving you?"

"Yes. She was tossing me over for—for you"

"Go on."

"We had this argument. It meant a lot to me. Publicity angles and all that." He changed to the other elbow. "I lost my head. I began to yell at her and I didn't look where I was driving. I ran into a guy. No damage—except the bumper and the windshield. The windshield shattered. Cornell found out about that and deduced the rest."

Ed Cornell had never told me this. Yet I remembered he had not accused me of having picked her up on Sunset— which had been the first police theory: he had stated I was waiting in the apartment when she came in. I was sick that Cornell was so far ahead of me; that these things which I had figured out *he* had known weeks ago! It was like a terrible race between us. But I was behind.

"You didn't hit her in the car—and kill her?"

"My God, no!" Robin said.

"After the accident what happened?"

"I took her home. She didn't have the key to her apartment. She said she usually got a pass key from the boy at the desk. But the switchboard was jammed and the boy was gone."

"Harry Williams wasn't there when you came in?"

"No."

"What did you do?"

"I—why don't you give me a cigarette?"

145

"I haven't any," I said.

"They're on the night stand. Will you hand me one?"

He lit up, propped himself against the pillow and went on. His tangled hair fell over his forehead.

"She said she knew a way to get in. We went upstairs, then out on the fire escape and crawled in the living-room windows. There're no screens on those windows, you know."

I was stunned. The windows *had* been open. His explanation was as good as mine, even better. And he had admitted these things to Ed Cornell. What did I have that was new? *Nothing!*

"Go on," I said.

"That's all. In the apartment we argued some more—and I left."

"Was Harry Williams downstairs when you went out?"

"No—the switchboard was empty."

I moved a little closer. "Isn't it true that after you and Vicky were in the apartment you lost your temper and hit her?"

"Hell, no!"

"I think you did."

He was trembling.

"You hit her—and you had that big metal ring on your finger. I haven't seen the ring since."

"Haven't you? Let me get up and I'll get it."

"All right."

I moved back and he got out of bed, crossed the room in his pajamas and opened a dresser drawer. He took out the ring and tossed it to me. Then he stood there with his hands on his hips.

"If I killed her that'd be Exhibit A—the weapon of murder. The most damning evidence against me anybody could get, so—I make you a gift of it!"

I turned the ring over in my hand.

"Would I do that," he said, "if I were guilty?"

I couldn't speak.

"I appreciate what you're trying to accomplish," he said. "Personally, I never did think you were guilty. None of us did. Hell, we were four guys who really wanted to promote

146

Vicky. We were just Hollywood people. We have our troubles. We cry a little, and love a little, but we don't go in for murder."

I started for the window. "I'm sorry I bothered you."

"It's all right. I won't tell them you were here."

My voice was hollow. "Where's Lanny Craig?"

"Gone to New York. I got a card from him. He says it's cold as hell."

"Hurd?"

"Still at the studio. But *they* aren't guilty, believe me!"

"*Somebody's* guilty," I said. "God, I—"

"Need any dough?"

"I could use some," I said.

Robin picked up his wallet, flipped it open and took out all that was there. It amounted to forty dollars. I stuck it in my blue jeans.

"Good luck," he said.

I drove the car down around the hills and on to Cahuenga. I kept driving. I meant to turn back but I kept driving. San Fernando fell behind me. The car ate up the black asphalt highway. I drove like the wind. My mind was turning the whole thing over. There were two of Ed Cornell's clues that bothered me. Vicky's shoe somebody had stood on and crushed. The cigarette that had been smashed out in the closet. Somebody had been hiding in the closet when she and Robin came in. *Who?* It had narrowed down to this. The answer of this one question contained the solution. I was suddenly possessed with the notion that I knew it.

The town of Doris in California is near the state line. It is a small town, and in the hotel where I had a room it was very hot. But I didn't spend much time in the hotel. Through the long days I stopped every person I met and asked endless questions. I didn't look at newspapers. I didn't want to know what they were doing with Jill. I couldn't stand to know.

At the end of the first week I found him.

It was on a Saturday night and it was raining very hard. There was a relentless crashing of thunder, and lightning streaked out of the sky. He lived in a ranch house ten miles

147

out of town. I stood there at the door and rapped my knuckles against it. After a long time the door opened and a woman peered out. She was withered, but very hard, with sharp, ugly little eyes.

"What is it you want?"

"I came to see Bill Hunter."

"Who are you?"

"I'm a friend of his from Doris."

"You don't work at the pool room?"

"No," I said.

She opened the door. "Come in, then. He's here in the living room."

I came in and she closed the door. He was sitting next to an open fire. He turned and looked up at me.

"Hello, Harry Williams," I said.

He stared at me. The old woman was his aunt and she was saying: "William gets in a lot of trouble at the pool room, don't you, William? How many times have I told you not to go there?" She talked to him as though he were not quite bright. But suddenly it struck her that I had spoken his real name, and she turned to me.

"What did you call him?"

"Harry Williams."

"But he's *not!* How foolish! He's—"

"He's Harry Williams."

"You—you knew him before?"

"Yes. Would you mind leaving the room for a moment?"

"No" she said. She folded her scrawny arms. "I won't leave the room at all."

Harry Williams was on his feet. Lightning flashed at the window, and the big yellow eyes behind the thick-lens glasses were horrible.

"How'd you get the name Hunter?" I said.

He watched me sullenly. His lips were ugly smears and his skin was bad. He shot a glance at his aunt.

She said: "When—ah—Harry came from—"

"From Hollywood," I said.

She pursed her lips. "Yes, from Hollywood—you see he came at a time when my son—Harry's second cousin—had gone away, joined the army. We were lonely here and we took him into our house. As a son. We just changed his name. It was easier that way for everybody."

"Except the police. And bright boy came here instead of going to his home up in Washington, or near any of his former friends—because he figured he'd never be traced. He laid low, and—"

She closed up. "Harry, who is this man?"

"He's from Hollywood," Williams said evenly. He couldn't take his eyes off me. They were hideous eyes like two small oranges.

I watched him. "You killed Vicky, didn't you?"

He didn't speak.

His aunt watched me. She must have known all about the murder.

"It was like this," I said. "When Lanny Craig left—you went back into the apartment to wait for Vicky. You intended to tell her about his visit."

"Yeah," he said. The lightning outside seemed to make him nervous.

"But you saw her coming in through the fire escape and Robin was with her. You weren't supposed to be hanging around in her apartment and you got scared. It was too late to make a break for the door—they'd have seen you. So you beat it into the bedroom. You hid in the closet! You smoked a cigarette in there and stood on one of her shoes."

"Yeah—yeah." There was sweat on his face.

"You heard her and Robin arguing. You heard the door slam when Robin left. You came out of the closet—"

"Stand clear, Harry!"

I turned. The old woman had a shotgun leveled at me. I didn't know where she had gotten it. Harry saw it.

"No! *Don't!* I'm not afraid. Let him go on. I *know* him!"

She lowered the gun but it was still pointed at me.

"Go on," Harry Williams said. "When you're through—there's something I want to say."

"You came out of the closet. Vicky saw you and screamed."

"Yeah."

"You were in love with her. You knew she'd signed a movie contract—was going to leave the apartment—"

It was as though he were transfixed. He nodded; now he began to talk.

"Yeah. She screamed, and yelled at me to get out. Her screaming got me excited. I went a little crazy maybe—listen, here's what I told her—I swear to God—I swear to God in heaven—I said, 'Vicky, you're going away. I want just one little kiss!' That's what I said. I told her I loved her." He was almost sobbing. "I only wanted one little kiss! But she kept screaming. I don't know why she was afraid of me—I tried to kiss her and she fought me and kept screaming!"

I wanted to vomit.

"I had that big iron key ring," he went on, "the ring with pass keys; I had it in my hand. I don't know what happened. I must have hit her. I think I caught her one along the side of the head. She went limp in my arms. Her eyes fluttered closed. I was all choked up. I dropped her. I began to scream. I ran out of the apartment. I got a freight train—I came back here to Doris. They hid me. We changed my name. You see—you see—"

The old lady slammed the shotgun down across the table. She wasn't going to use it. "Harry, you're a fool!" she said.

"What's the difference?" he said. "The cops figured this all out. They found me. They just said lay low and don't talk about the murder. They understood how it was—how I just wanted to kiss her. This guy'll understand, too. I didn't mean to hunt her, I just—"

"What was it you said?"

"I said the cops, they—"

"Cops?"

"Well, no—just one detective by himself. I suppose he told the others how it was. He was a guy from L.A., this detective. His name was—"

It was noon. In Los Angeles the traffic was thick on the streets and the sidewalks were crowded with people. I was in an old hotel. I knocked at the door of a room. Then I went in. I let the door slam behind me.

Ed Cornell looked up.

Chapter Twenty-Three

"Hello, Operator Thirteen," I said.

He wore white pajamas. They were wet with sweat, and they were soiled. In the shadow that fell across the room from the window his face was long and evil. He had cards laid out in a game of solitaire. He had been putting down a card and his hand stopped in mid-air. His face was jaundiced, sickly, and his eyes were a burning red. He was running a fever—and I knew somehow that he was on his last legs.

There were six different pictures of Vicky around the walls. They were large size. Three of them were intimate pictures. In four of them she seemed to be looking at you. I felt cold. It was as though I were walking over her grave. On the dresser I saw items of her clothing. There were three half-used bottles of her perfume. I saw a diary and telegrams and letters which should have been in police files, not here. But I could not get rid of the feeling that Vicky had her eyes on me. That from the walls she was looking at me. To be in this room was like living with her.

I remembered all of the things Ed Cornell had said. Harry Williams couldn't be guilty. Jealousy was the only strong motive. *Jealousy.* Rank, bitter hatred. The blind obsession of a man about to die. With each day his hatred for me had grown. It was very clear now. The whole picture was there. The morning he had stood on the corner at dawn and watched as I brought Jill home. His scorn was acid that day. He must have imagined I'd violated Vicky's tomb!

What profane, what lewd, sick thoughts must have brewed in his mind, stirred agony in his withered soul, as he sat here day after day in his self-made aura of Vicky Lynn! His subconscious flaying and screaming against the impotence which twisted him. I was an object, a figure, a symbol, even an effigy at which to hurl the bitter gall from the exploded bladder of his ego!

For weeks he alone had been fully aware of the fact that Harry Williams was the murderer!

It didn't matter! He arrested me for murder while Williams' confession still rang in his ears! He knew what he was doing. It was not the law I was fleeing—but him. The relentless pursuer! He would haunt me, hound me, persecute me until I hung from the end of a rope. The knowledge of my innocence only fed flame to his fury. He meant to destroy me. He had trumped up a case—manufactured evidence.

And all the time he knew that Harry Williams was guilty.

It was only in the very beginning that he must have honestly believed I was the killer. He was too good a detective to hold that opinion long. He alone had uncovered the genuine solution—a solution to which he deliberately closed his eyes.

I had heard Vicky say months ago that Harry Williams had complained about his job and said he could always get employment in Doris, California—that he had a second cousin up there. Williams had told this to no one but Vicky. She was dead. He was not overly bright but he realized that the police would find his home address without difficulty and would check with every known friend he'd ever had. But the place in Doris was an ace up his sleeve; and this only because his cousin had recently dropped him a card to the effect that fruit pickers were needed up there. Probably a hundred such cards were sent out to every address the cousin (now in the army) could find. When the fruit is ripe, or a week or so earlier, certain ranchers do this. But for Harry Williams it was obscurity. His cousin was such a distant relative that it wasn't likely he'd be traced to him. He went to Doris, was welcomed by a shrewd, mean and lonely old woman, who saw in him a likeness to her son who, on a sudden, impulsive decision, had enlisted in the army. She had wrung a confession from Harry, and had connived to keep him hidden. Doris was a very small town, but until the clamor died down Harry never even left the ranch. It was only after Ed Cornell discovered him, seemingly cleared him, that he had started visiting the Doris pool room. There, with his new name, weeks after most of the active hunt for him had died down, no one paid any attention to him. No other law officer (if indeed, in a place so small he even passed one by) recognized him as Harry Williams.

Ed Cornell with only one possible clue: the post card from Harry's cousin which might have been left in his room the night he fled, had journeyed alone to Doris, discovered Harry without difficulty, and heard his confession. And for what must have been the first time in Cornell's life—turned his back on a murderer.

Cornell warned Williams to keep his mouth shut, and gambled on the chance that no one else would ever find Williams. At least, until after I'd been executed. If he was discovered then—by accident some day—it was of no importance. Ed Cornell knew that his own days were numbered and he cared nothing for the fact that it would be revealed he had deliberately sent an innocent man to the gallows. It was even likely that by the time all this happened Cornell himself, as sick as he was, would have died. But he wanted first the satisfaction of seeing me executed. His was the most fantastic game in the world: he wanted to commit a legal murder! He wanted the state to be his assassins!

Even now, with my appearance in this room, he labored under the impression that his plans were moving with flawless precision. He imagined that he had cornered me—that I was in a trap from which there was no possible escape. It would give him a certain, exquisite pleasure to see me squirm. Cat and mouse. It had never occurred to him that I could track down Harry Williams; that through him I could acquit myself. And Harry Williams? He was only the murderer. It was Ed Cornell who was the villain of this piece!

I should have known. I should have guessed when he pressed the charge he did against Jill. When out of his own pocket he posted the reward money. . . . *"I'll fry you in oil. . . . You'll never escape!"*

He laid the card down now. He sat very still. I heard the sound of the clock; and I could hear the downtown traffic. The air of the room was foul. All of the windows were shut.

He spoke, as though he were talking to the cards.

"Come to give yourself up? I knew you'd be back! I suppose you want to make a deal—you'll surrender if I let the girl go." He looked at me coldly. "I suppose you came here to be noble. Well, it's no good!"

I did not move.

"You'll excuse me if I don't get up," he said. "The doctor's got me in bed. They want me to go to a sanitarium, see? But you wouldn't be interested, would you?"

He was catching for his breath. He hated me so thoroughly he could no longer cover it up.

"Well, what the hell *do* you want?"

"I was talking to Harry Williams," I said.

His face was expressionless. But his eyes went chill. He looked down at the cards.

"I heard the confession," I said, "and *you* heard it—weeks ago, and yet—" I could feel Vicky's eyes staring down. "You were still determined to send me to the gas chamber, and you—"

I stopped. The room was silent. He began mixing the cards. Suddenly he leapt from the bed and toward a table. I grabbed him and slammed him back across the bed. The moment he fell he was seized with a fit of coughing. He lay there, that cough racking his throat, retching through his decayed lungs. His police gun was on the table. He hadn't reached it. I didn't go near it.

At last he stopped coughing. He wiped his mouth with a handkerchief. He spoke.

"Well?"

"Nothing," I said. "There's no words. It's over. I'm released. The game between us is finished."

He just watched me. I turned. One by one I ripped the pictures of Vicky from off the wall. I tore them into bits. I broke the perfume bottles in the waste basket. Then I leaned back against the dresser. I was breathing hard.

"This is over, too, Cornell. You're—alone now."

His eyes dropped. He looked at his hands. He was sitting on the edge of the bed, his pajamas hanging loose on his thin body.

"Call the D. A.," he said. "Tell him to come over here."

How do you say *the end*? What are the words you use? For there is no end, really. There are simply episodes, and all of the episodes put together make one lifetime. It's rather wonderful! The earth is sweet and green after the rain, and that is the way with laughter after tears. I remember I could not end the first play I wrote because I felt the drama was but a particle of the lives of the people in it, and they should go on. I cannot end this.

Ed Cornell told the whole story to the District Attorney and Jill was released. Ed Cornell did not elaborate.

He offered no excuse for himself, and I made no charge against him. Two weeks ago he died of tuberculosis in a sanitarium in Arizona. In his effects they found a bent and worn picture of Vicky Lynn. I don't know how he got it. Harry Williams was arrested in Doris, California, and sentenced to life in San Quentin.

So the end did not come violently. It was all gradual. The Williams trial. The death of Cornell. And that day in Santa Barbara when Jill and I were married in an old Spanish mission. There are so many things! The opening of my first picture *Winter in Paris,* and the nice house beside the sea where Jill and I live. All of these things have become reality, but if this were a screen play I think I'd go back—back to that day Cornell confessed—and write the Fade Out with the scene, of Jill's release from jail.

It was late afternoon, and the sun shone dimly on the gray stone steps. Pigeons strutted up and down, and people were coming and going. Jill came out, wearing a tan skirt that was tight on her hips, and the sandals with red cork heels. She came down the steps, and she saw me.

"Why, darling," she said, "you've shaved!"

I was holding her in my arms then and it was very hard for me to speak. I just held her close, and finally I said:

"Hello, mommy!"

BLACK LIZARD BOOKS

JIM THOMPSON
  AFTER DARK, MY SWEET $3.95
  THE ALCOHOLICS $3.95
  THE CRIMINAL $3.95
  CROPPER'S CABIN $3.95
  THE GETAWAY $3.95
  THE GRIFTERS $3.95
  A HELL OF A WOMAN $3.95
  NOTHING MORE THAN MURDER $3.95
  POP. 1280 $3.95
  RECOIL $3.95
  SAVAGE NIGHT $3.95
  A SWELL LOOKING BABE $3.95
  WILD TOWN $3.95

HARRY WHITTINGTON
  THE DEVIL WEARS WINGS $3.95
  FIRES THAT DESTROY $4.95
  FORGIVE ME, KILLER $3.95
  A MOMENT TO PREY $4.95
  A TICKET TO HELL $3.95
  WEB OF MURDER $3.95

CHARLES WILLEFORD
  THE BURNT ORANGE HERESY $3.95
  COCKFIGHTER $3.95
  PICK-UP $3.95

ROBERT EDMOND ALTER
  CARNY KILL $3.95
  SWAMP SISTER $3.95

W.L. HEATH
  ILL WIND $3.95
  VIOLENT SATURDAY $3.95

PAUL CAIN
  FAST ONE $3.95
  SEVEN SLAYERS $3.95

FREDRIC BROWN
  HIS NAME WAS DEATH $3.95
  THE FAR CRY $3.95

DAVID GOODIS
  BLACK FRIDAY $3.95
  CASSIDY'S GIRL $3.95
  NIGHTFALL $3.95
  SHOOT THE PIANO PLAYER $3.95
  STREET OF NO RETURN $3.95

HELEN NIELSEN
  DETOUR $4.95
  SING ME A MURDER $4.95

DAN J. MARLOWE
  *THE NAME OF THE GAME
  IS DEATH* $4.95
  NEVER LIVE TWICE $4.95

MURRAY SINCLAIR
  ONLY IN L.A. $4.95
  TOUGH LUCK L.A. $4.95

AND OTHERS . . .
  FRANCIS CARCO • *PERVERSITY* $3.95
  BARRY GIFFORD • *PORT TROPIQUE* $3.95
  NJAMI SIMON • *COFFIN & CO.* $3.95
  ERIC KNIGHT (RICHARD HALLAS) • *YOU PLAY THE BLACK
    AND THE RED COMES UP* $3.95
  GERTRUDE STEIN • *BLOOD ON THE DINING ROOM FLOOR* $6.95
  KENT NELSON • *THE STRAIGHT MAN* $3.50
  JIM NISBET • *THE DAMNED DON'T DIE* $3.95
  STEVE FISHER • *I WAKE UP SCREAMING* $4.95
  LIONEL WHITE • *THE KILLING* $4.95
  THE BLACK LIZARD ANTHOLOGY OF CRIME FICTION
    Edited by **EDWARD GORMAN** $8.95

HARDCOVER ORIGINALS:
  LETHAL INJECTION by **JIM NISBET** $15.95
  GOODBYE L.A. by **MURRAY SINCLAIR** $15.95
